ANNO[illegible]G ORANGE™

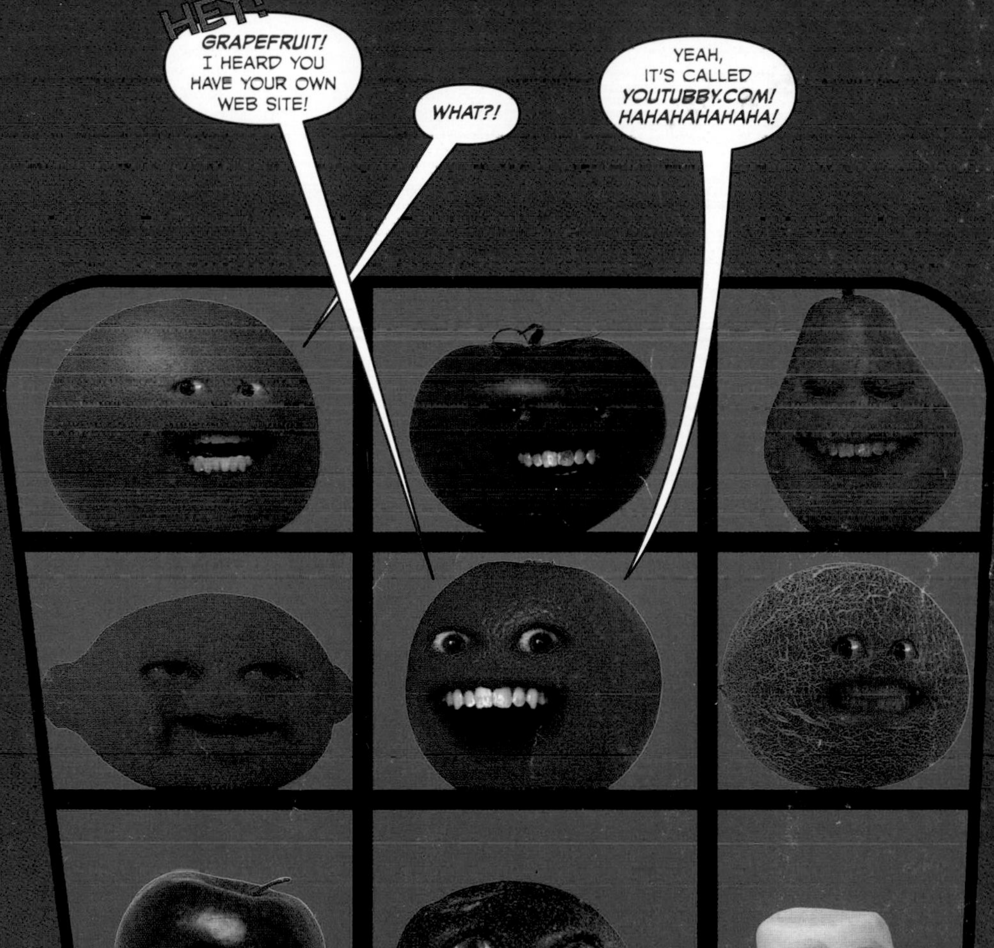
HEY! GRAPEFRUIT! I HEARD YOU HAVE YOUR OWN WEB SITE!
WHAT?!
YEAH, IT'S CALLED YOUTUBBY.COM! HAHAHAHAHAHA!

PAPERCUTZ™

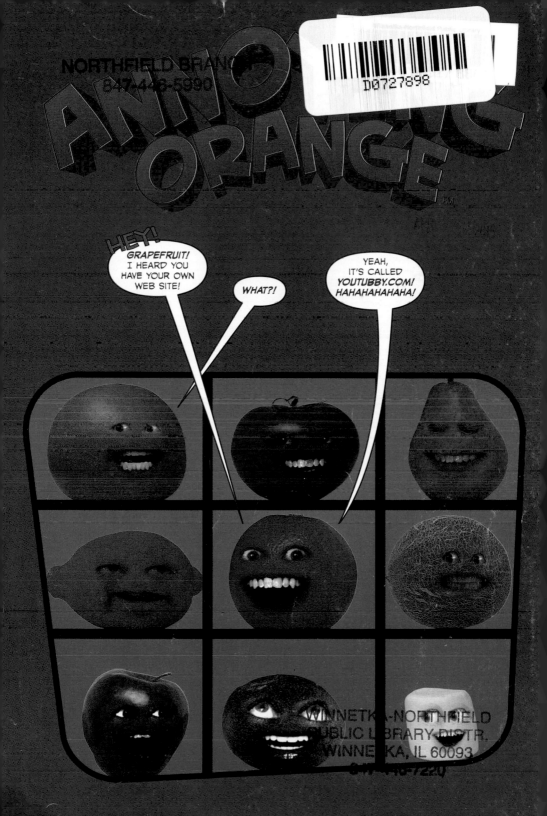

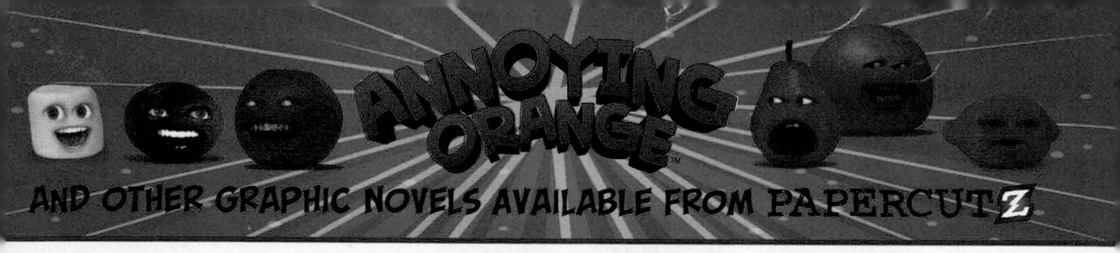
ANNOYING ORANGE
AND OTHER GRAPHIC NOVELS AVAILABLE FROM PAPERCUTZ

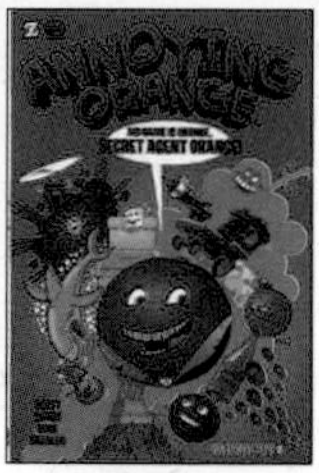
ANNOYING ORANGE

ANNOYING ORANGE
Graphic Novel #1
"Secret Agent Orange"

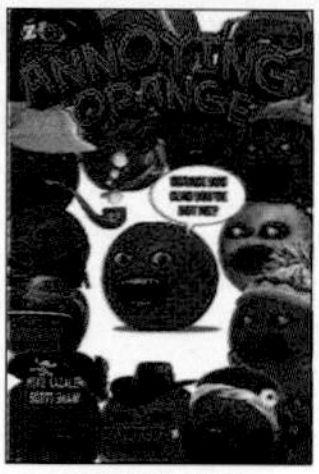
ANNOYING ORANGE

ANNOYING ORANGE
Graphic Novel #2
"Orange You Glad You're Not Me?"

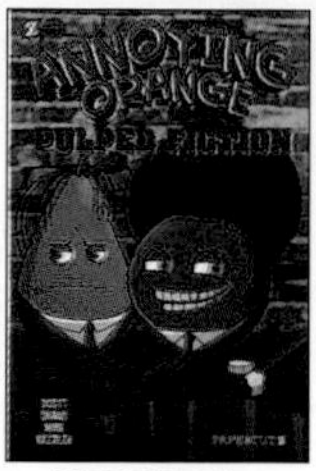
ANNOYING ORANGE

ANNOYING ORANGE
Graphic Novel #3
"Pulped Fiction"

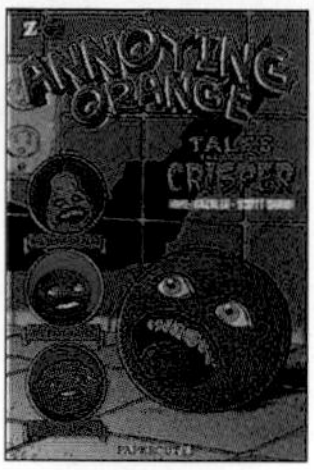
ANNOYING ORANGE

ANNOYING ORANGE
Graphic Novel #4
"Tales from the Crisper"

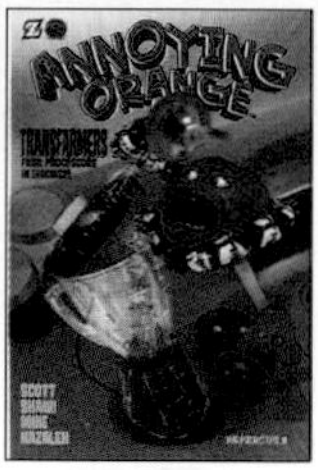
ANNOYING ORANGE

ANNOYING ORANGE
Graphic Novel #5
"Transfarmers: Food Processors in Disguise!"

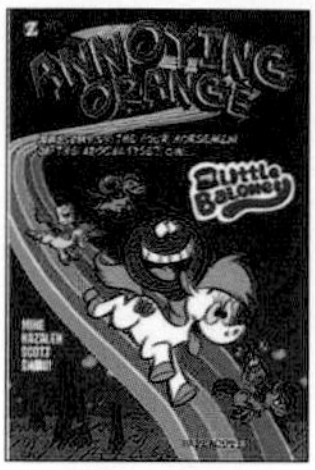
ANNOYING ORANGE

ANNOYING ORANGE
Graphic Novel #6
"My Little Baloney"

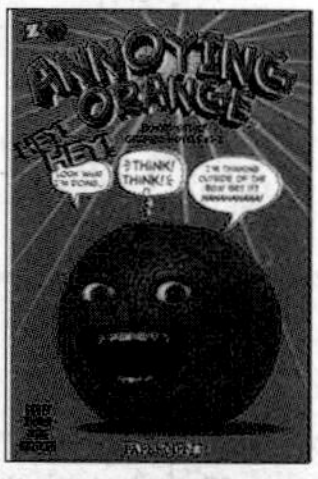
ANNOYING ORANGE

ANNOYING ORANGE BOXED SET
Featuring ANNOYING ORANGE #1– 3

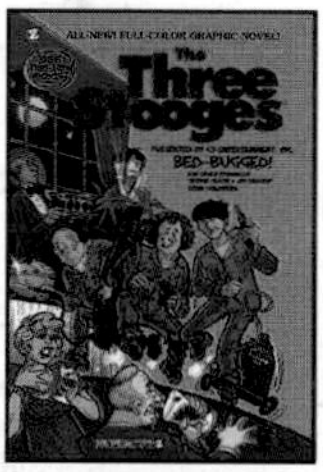
The Three Stooges

THE THREE STOOGES #1
"Bed-Bugged!"

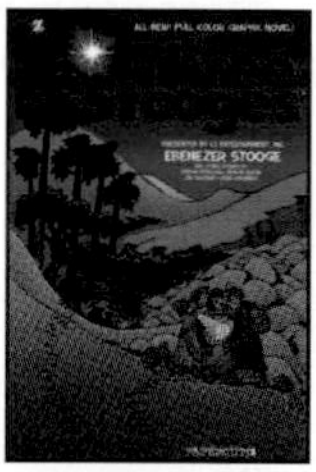

THE THREE STOOGES #2
"Ebenezer Stooge"

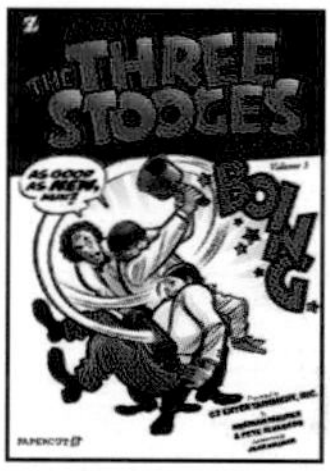
THE THREE STOOGES

THE BEST OF THE THREE STOOGES COMICBOOKS Vol. 1

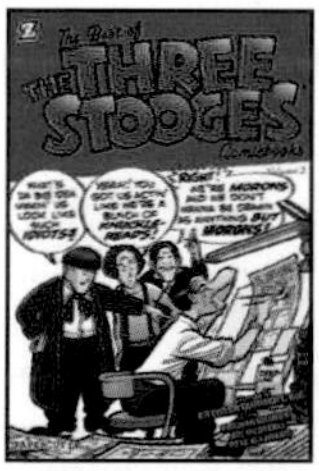
THE THREE STOOGES

THE BEST OF THE THREE STOOGES COMICBOOKS Vol. 2

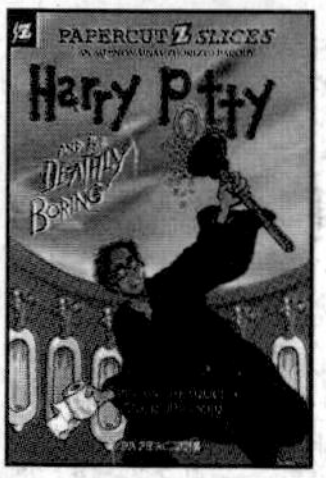
PAPERCUTZ SLICES
Harry Potty

PAPERCUTZ SLICES
Graphic Novel #1
"Harry Potty and the Deathly Boring"

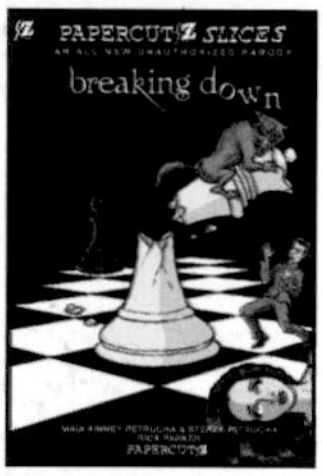
PAPERCUTZ SLICES
breaking down

PAPERCUTZ SLICES
Graphic Novel #2
"Breaking Down"

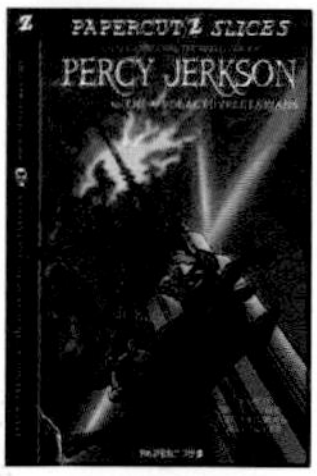
PAPERCUTZ SLICES
PERCY JERKSON

PAPERCUTZ SLICES
Graphic Novel #3
"Percy Jerkson & The Ovolactovegetarians"

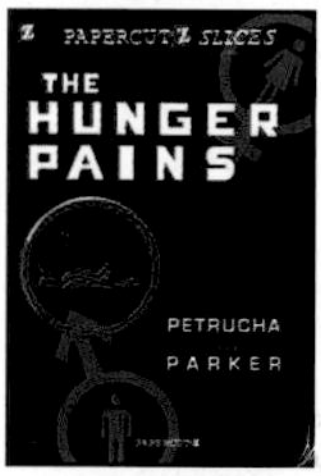
PAPERCUTZ SLICES
THE HUNGER PAINS
PETRUCHA
PARKER

PAPERCUTZ SLICES
Graphic Novel #4
"The Hunger Pains"

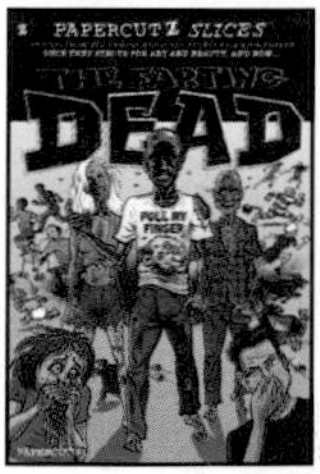
PAPERCUTZ SLICES
THE FARTING DEAD

PAPERCUTZ SLICES
Graphic Novel #5
"The Farting Dead"

ANNOYING ORANGE, ANNOYING ORANGE BOXED SET and PAPERCUTZ SLICES graphic novels, the print editions, are still available at booksellers everywhere.

Or order directly from Papercutz. ANNOYING ORANGE, PAPERCUTZ SLICES, and THE THREE STOOGES are available in paperback for $6.99 each; in hardcover for $10.99, except ANNOYING ORANGE #2, hardcover is $11.99, and ANNOYING ORANGE #3, #4, and #5 are $7.99 paperback, and $11.99 hardcover. ANNOYING ORANGE BOXED SET (featuring paperbacks of ANNOYING ORANGE #1-3) is $19.99. THE BEST OF THE THREE STOOGES COMICBOOKS are available only in hardcover for $19.99 each. Please add $4.00 for postage and handling for the first book, and add $1.00 for each additional book.
Make check payable to NBM Publishing.

Send to: Papercutz, 160 Broadway, Suite 700, East Wing, New York, NY 10038

Or call 800 886 1223 (9-6 EST M-F) MC-Visa-Amex accepted

papercutz.com

ANNOYING ORANGE and PAPERCUTZ SLICES graphic novels are also available digitally wherever e-books are sold.

ANNOYING ORANGE™

My Little Baloney

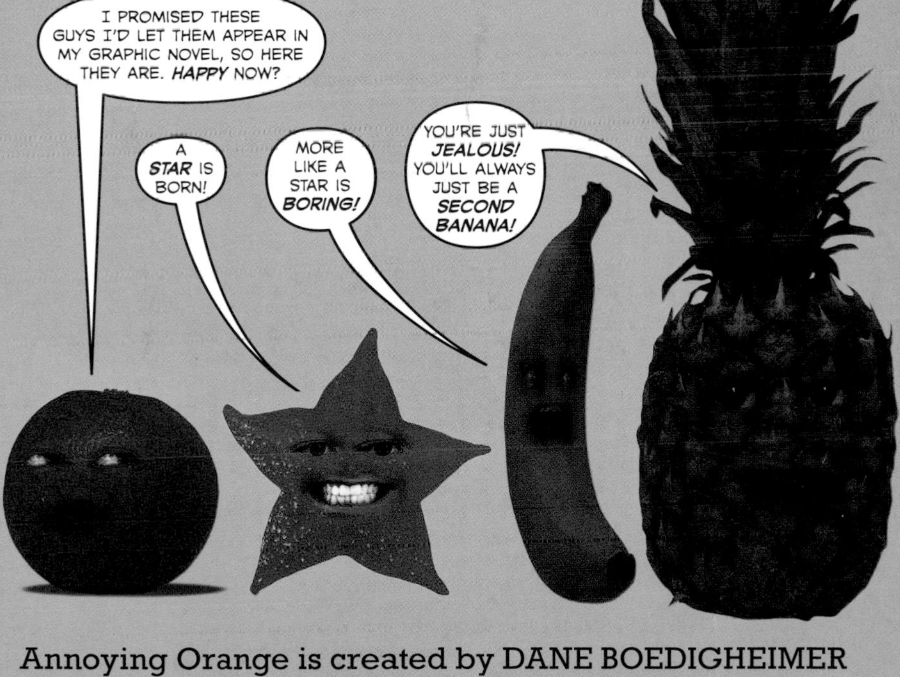
I PROMISED THESE GUYS I'D LET THEM APPEAR IN MY GRAPHIC NOVEL, SO HERE THEY ARE. *HAPPY* NOW?
A *STAR* IS BORN!
MORE LIKE A STAR IS *BORING!*
YOU'RE JUST *JEALOUS!* YOU'LL ALWAYS JUST BE A *SECOND BANANA!*

Annoying Orange is created by DANE BOEDIGHEIMER

SCOTT SHAW! – Writer & Artist

MIKE KAZALEH – Writer & Artist

LAURIE E. SMITH – Colorist

PAPERCUTZ™

New York

entouorange
100% annoying

ANNOYING ORANGE™

#6 "My Little Baloney"

"Fruitstones, Meet the Fruitstones!"
Scott Shaw! – Writer & Artist
Laurie E. Smith – Colorist
Chris Nelson – Letterer

"My Little Baloney"
Mike Kazaleh – Writer & Artist
Laurie E. Smith – Colorist
Chris Nelson – Letterer

Mike Kazaleh – Cover Artist

Special Thanks to: Gary Binkow, Tim Blankley, Dane Boedigheimer, Spencer Grove, Teresa Harris, Reza Izad, Debra Joester, Polina Rey, Tom Sheppard
Production Coordinator: Beth Scorzato
Associate Editor: Michael Petranek
Jim Salicrup
Editor-in-Chief

ISBN: 978-1-59707-733-0 paperback edition
ISBN: 978-1-59707-734-7 hardcover edition

TM & © 2014 Annoying Orange, Inc.
Used under license by 14th Hour Productions, LLC.
Editorial matter Copyright © 2014 by Papercutz.

Printed in China
October 2014 by O.G. Printing Productions LTD.
Units 2 & 3, 5/F Lemmi Centre
59 Hoi Yuen Road
Kwon Tong, Kowloon

Distributed by Macmillan
First Printing

MEET THE FRUIT...

ORANGE

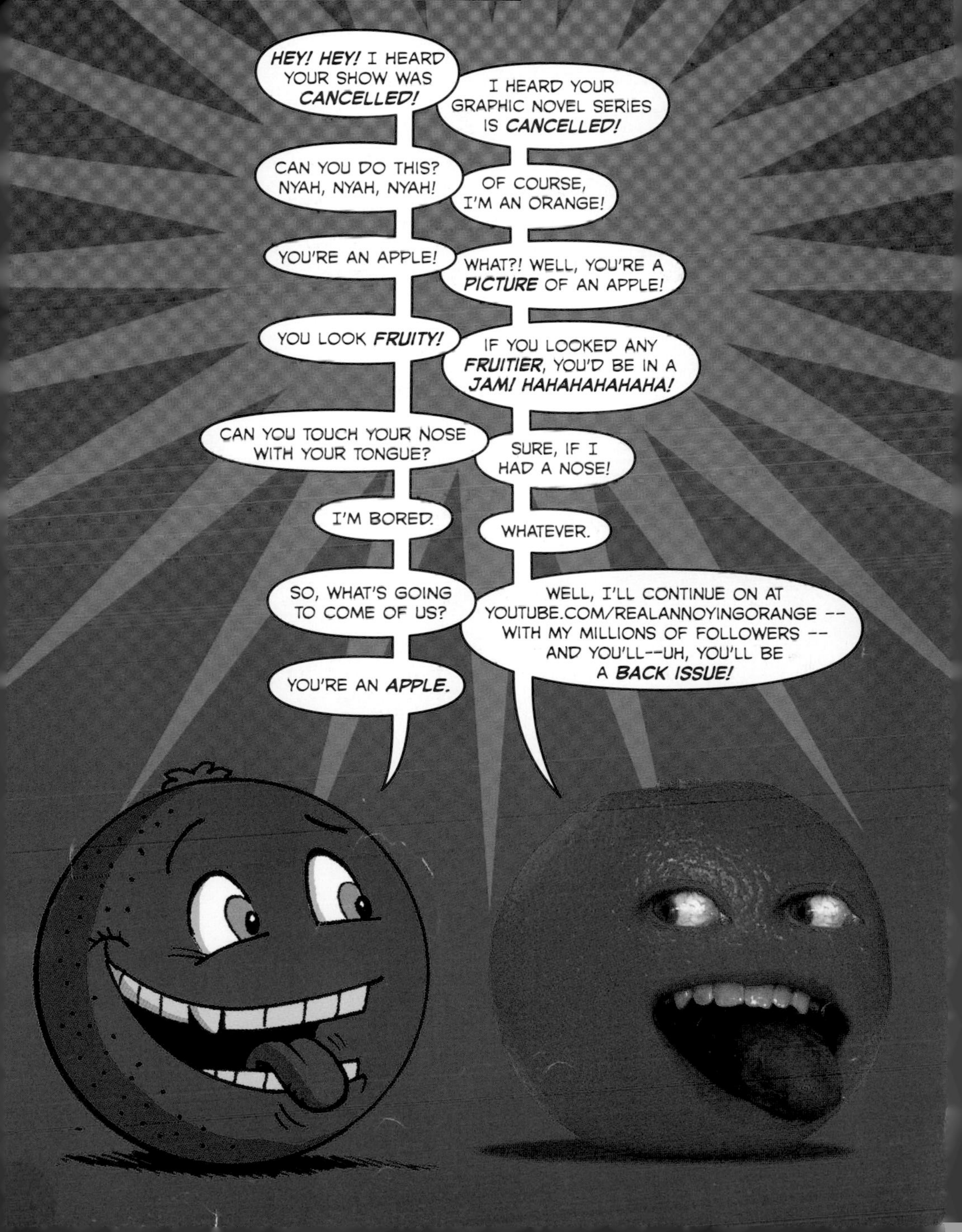
HEY! HEY! I HEARD YOUR SHOW WAS CANCELLED!
I HEARD YOUR GRAPHIC NOVEL SERIES IS CANCELLED!
CAN YOU DO THIS? NYAH, NYAH, NYAH!
OF COURSE, I'M AN ORANGE!
YOU'RE AN APPLE!
WHAT?! WELL, YOU'RE A PICTURE OF AN APPLE!
YOU LOOK FRUITY!
IF YOU LOOKED ANY FRUITIER, YOU'D BE IN A JAM! HAHAHAHAHAHA!
CAN YOU TOUCH YOUR NOSE WITH YOUR TONGUE?
SURE, IF I HAD A NOSE!
I'M BORED.
WHATEVER.
SO, WHAT'S GOING TO COME OF US?
WELL, I'LL CONTINUE ON AT YOUTUBE.COM/REALANNOYINGORANGE -- WITH MY MILLIONS OF FOLLOWERS -- AND YOU'LL--UH, YOU'LL BE A BACK ISSUE!
YOU'RE AN APPLE.

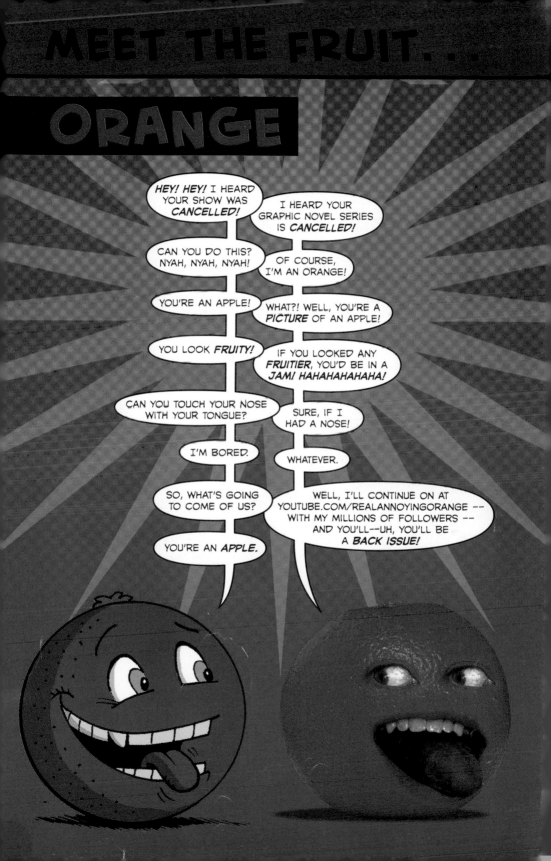

PEAR

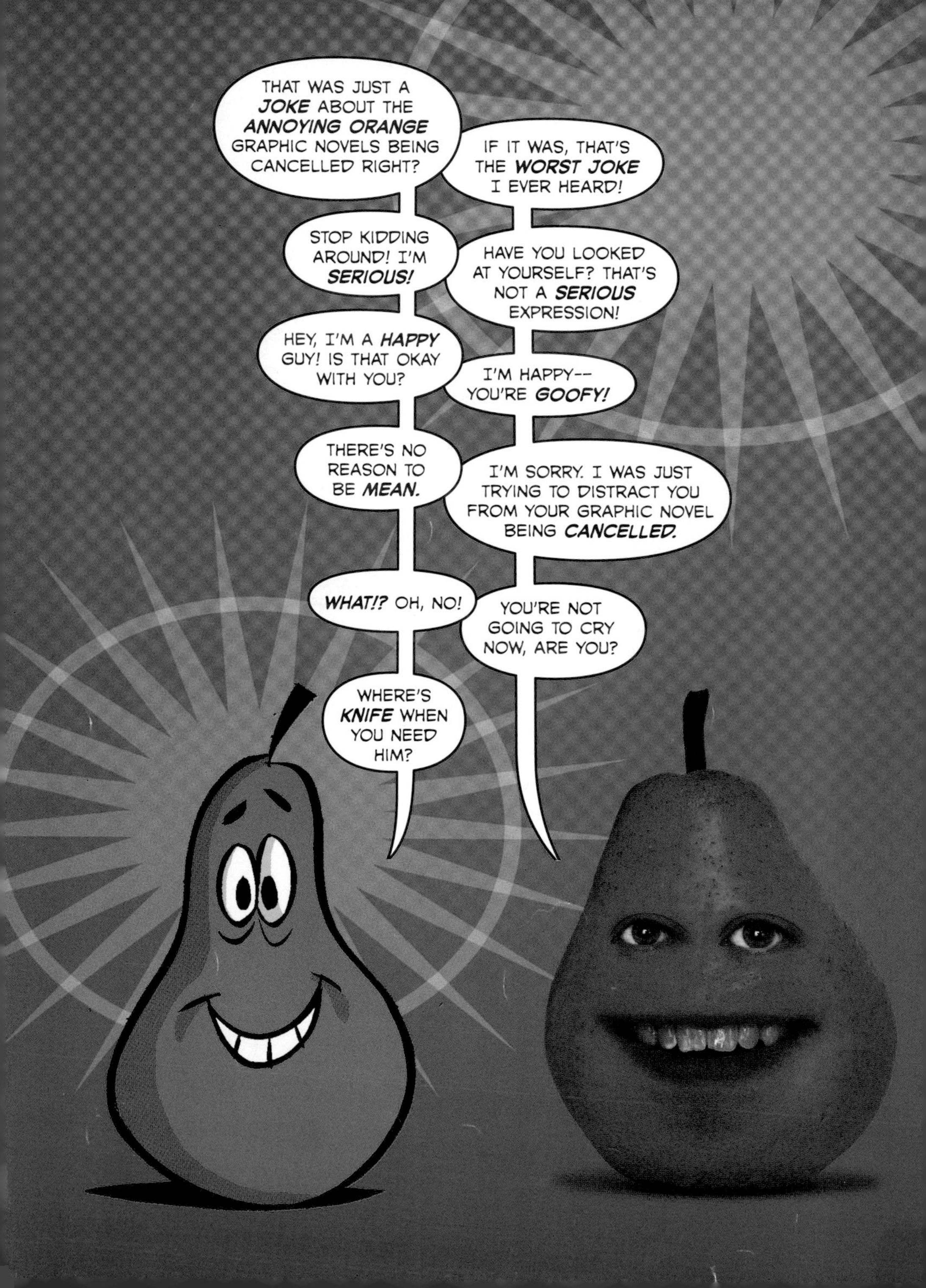

THAT WAS JUST A JOKE ABOUT THE ANNOYING ORANGE GRAPHIC NOVELS BEING CANCELLED RIGHT?
IF IT WAS, THAT'S THE WORST JOKE I EVER HEARD!
STOP KIDDING AROUND! I'M SERIOUS!
HAVE YOU LOOKED AT YOURSELF? THAT'S NOT A SERIOUS EXPRESSION!
HEY, I'M A HAPPY GUY! IS THAT OKAY WITH YOU?
I'M HAPPY-- YOU'RE GOOFY!
THERE'S NO REASON TO BE MEAN.
I'M SORRY. I WAS JUST TRYING TO DISTRACT YOU FROM YOUR GRAPHIC NOVEL BEING CANCELLED.
WHAT!? OH, NO!
YOU'RE NOT GOING TO CRY NOW, ARE YOU?
WHERE'S KNIFE WHEN YOU NEED HIM?

MARSHMALLOW

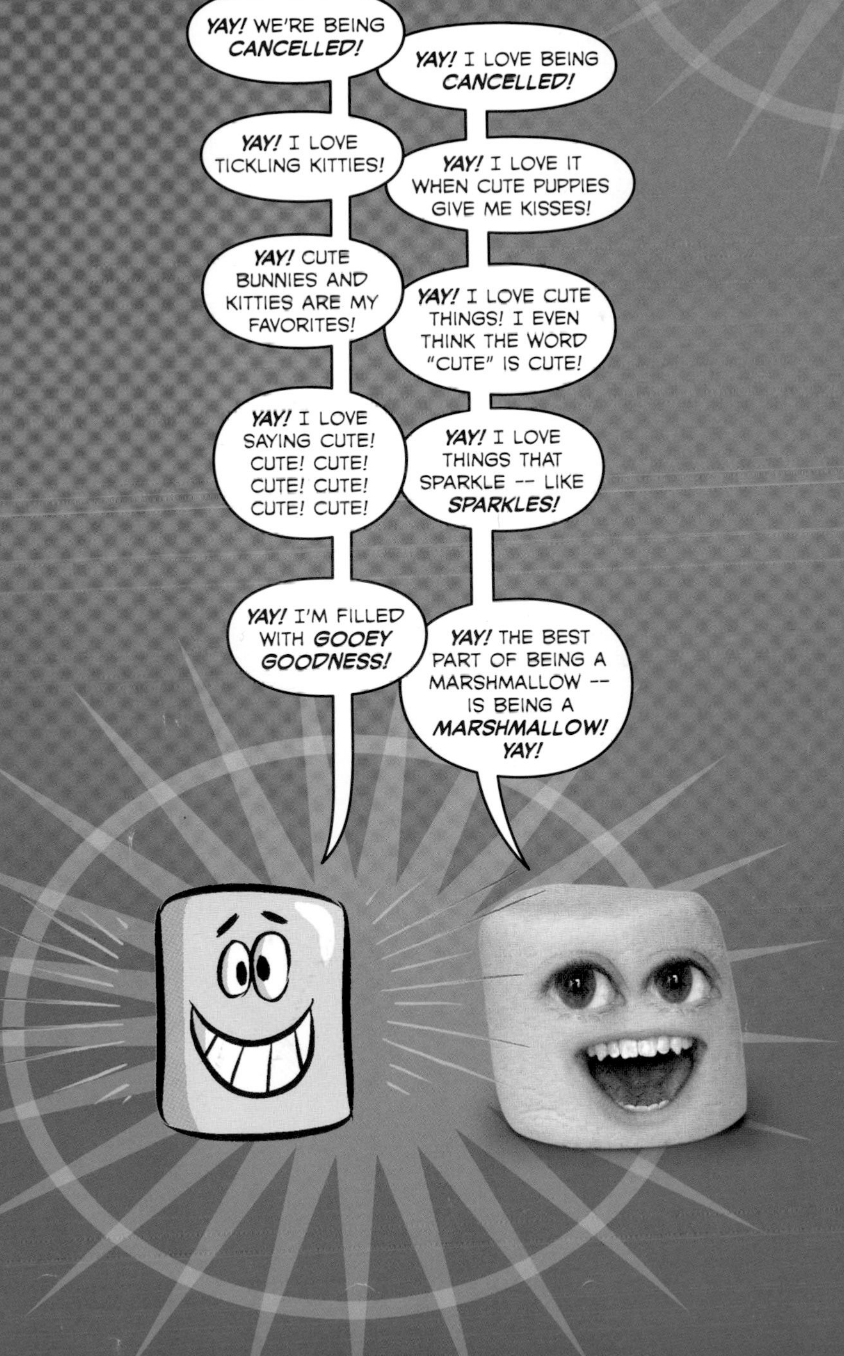
YAY! WE'RE BEING CANCELLED!
YAY! I LOVE BEING CANCELLED!
YAY! I LOVE TICKLING KITTIES!
YAY! I LOVE IT WHEN CUTE PUPPIES GIVE ME KISSES!
YAY! CUTE BUNNIES AND KITTIES ARE MY FAVORITES!
YAY! I LOVE CUTE THINGS! I EVEN THINK THE WORD "CUTE" IS CUTE!
YAY! I LOVE SAYING CUTE! CUTE! CUTE! CUTE! CUTE! CUTE! CUTE!
YAY! I LOVE THINGS THAT SPARKLE -- LIKE SPARKLES!
YAY! I'M FILLED WITH GOOEY GOODNESS!
YAY! THE BEST PART OF BEING A MARSHMALLOW -- IS BEING A MARSHMALLOW! YAY!

PASSION FRUIT

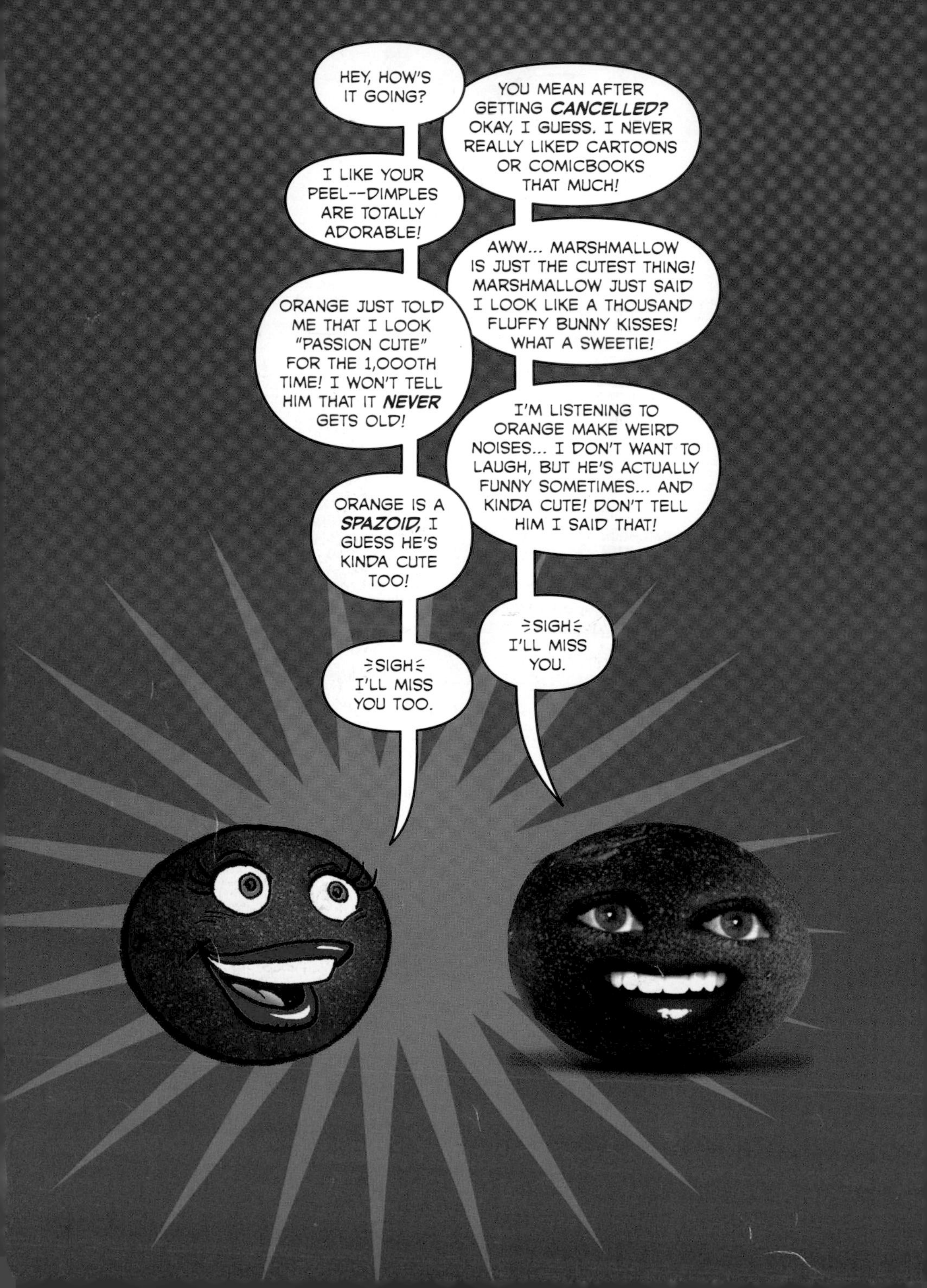
HEY, HOW'S IT GOING?
YOU MEAN AFTER GETTING ***CANCELLED?*** OKAY, I GUESS. I NEVER REALLY LIKED CARTOONS OR COMICBOOKS THAT MUCH!
I LIKE YOUR PEEL--DIMPLES ARE TOTALLY ADORABLE!
AWW... MARSHMALLOW IS JUST THE CUTEST THING! MARSHMALLOW JUST SAID I LOOK LIKE A THOUSAND FLUFFY BUNNY KISSES! WHAT A SWEETIE!
ORANGE JUST TOLD ME THAT I LOOK "PASSION CUTE" FOR THE 1,000TH TIME! I WON'T TELL HIM THAT IT ***NEVER*** GETS OLD!
I'M LISTENING TO ORANGE MAKE WEIRD NOISES... I DON'T WANT TO LAUGH, BUT HE'S ACTUALLY FUNNY SOMETIMES... AND KINDA CUTE! DON'T TELL HIM I SAID THAT!
ORANGE IS A ***SPAZOID,*** I GUESS HE'S KINDA CUTE TOO!
SIGH I'LL MISS YOU.
SIGH I'LL MISS YOU TOO.

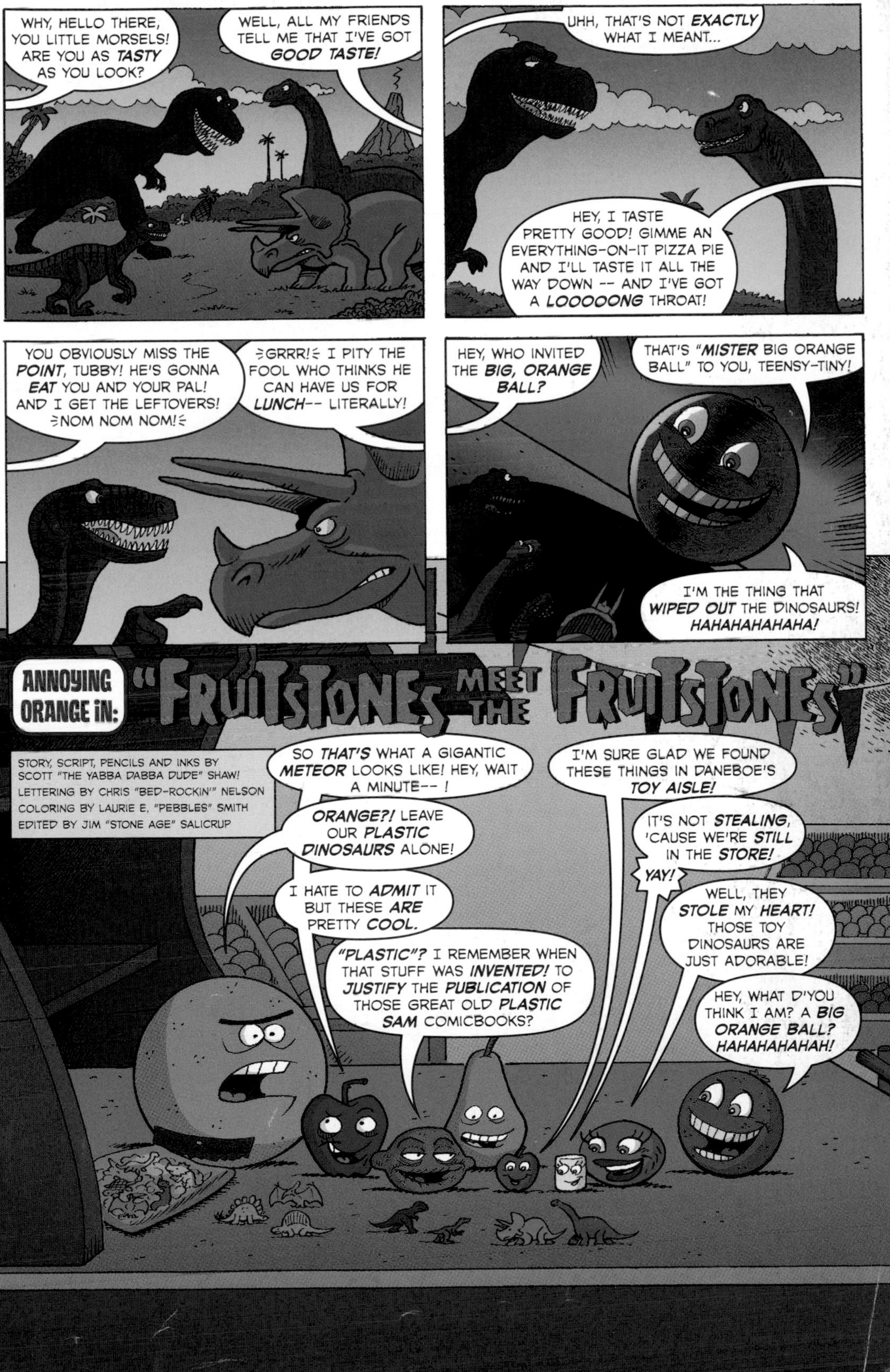
WHY, HELLO THERE, YOU LITTLE MORSELS! ARE YOU AS TASTY AS YOU LOOK?
WELL, ALL MY FRIENDS TELL ME THAT I'VE GOT GOOD TASTE!
UHH, THAT'S NOT EXACTLY WHAT I MEANT...
HEY, I TASTE PRETTY GOOD! GIMME AN EVERYTHING-ON-IT PIZZA PIE AND I'LL TASTE IT ALL THE WAY DOWN -- AND I'VE GOT A LOOOOONG THROAT!
YOU OBVIOUSLY MISS THE POINT, TUBBY! HE'S GONNA EAT YOU AND YOUR PAL! AND I GET THE LEFTOVERS! NOM NOM NOM!
GRRR! I PITY THE FOOL WHO THINKS HE CAN HAVE US FOR LUNCH-- LITERALLY!
HEY, WHO INVITED THE BIG, ORANGE BALL?
THAT'S "MISTER BIG ORANGE BALL" TO YOU, TEENSY-TINY!
I'M THE THING THAT WIPED OUT THE DINOSAURS! HAHAHAHAHAHA!
ANNOYING ORANGE IN:
"FRUITSTONES MEET THE FRUITSTONES"
STORY, SCRIPT, PENCILS AND INKS BY SCOTT "THE YABBA DABBA DUDE" SHAW!
LETTERING BY CHRIS "BED-ROCKIN'" NELSON
COLORING BY LAURIE E. "PEBBLES" SMITH
EDITED BY JIM "STONE AGE" SALICRUP
SO THAT'S WHAT A GIGANTIC METEOR LOOKS LIKE! HEY, WAIT A MINUTE-- !
ORANGE?! LEAVE OUR PLASTIC DINOSAURS ALONE!
I HATE TO ADMIT IT BUT THESE ARE PRETTY COOL.
"PLASTIC"? I REMEMBER WHEN THAT STUFF WAS INVENTED! TO JUSTIFY THE PUBLICATION OF THOSE GREAT OLD PLASTIC SAM COMICBOOKS?
I'M SURE GLAD WE FOUND THESE THINGS IN DANEBOE'S TOY AISLE!
IT'S NOT STEALING, 'CAUSE WE'RE STILL IN THE STORE!
YAY!
WELL, THEY STOLE MY HEART! THOSE TOY DINOSAURS ARE JUST ADORABLE!
HEY, WHAT D'YOU THINK I AM? A BIG ORANGE BALL? HAHAHAHAHAH!

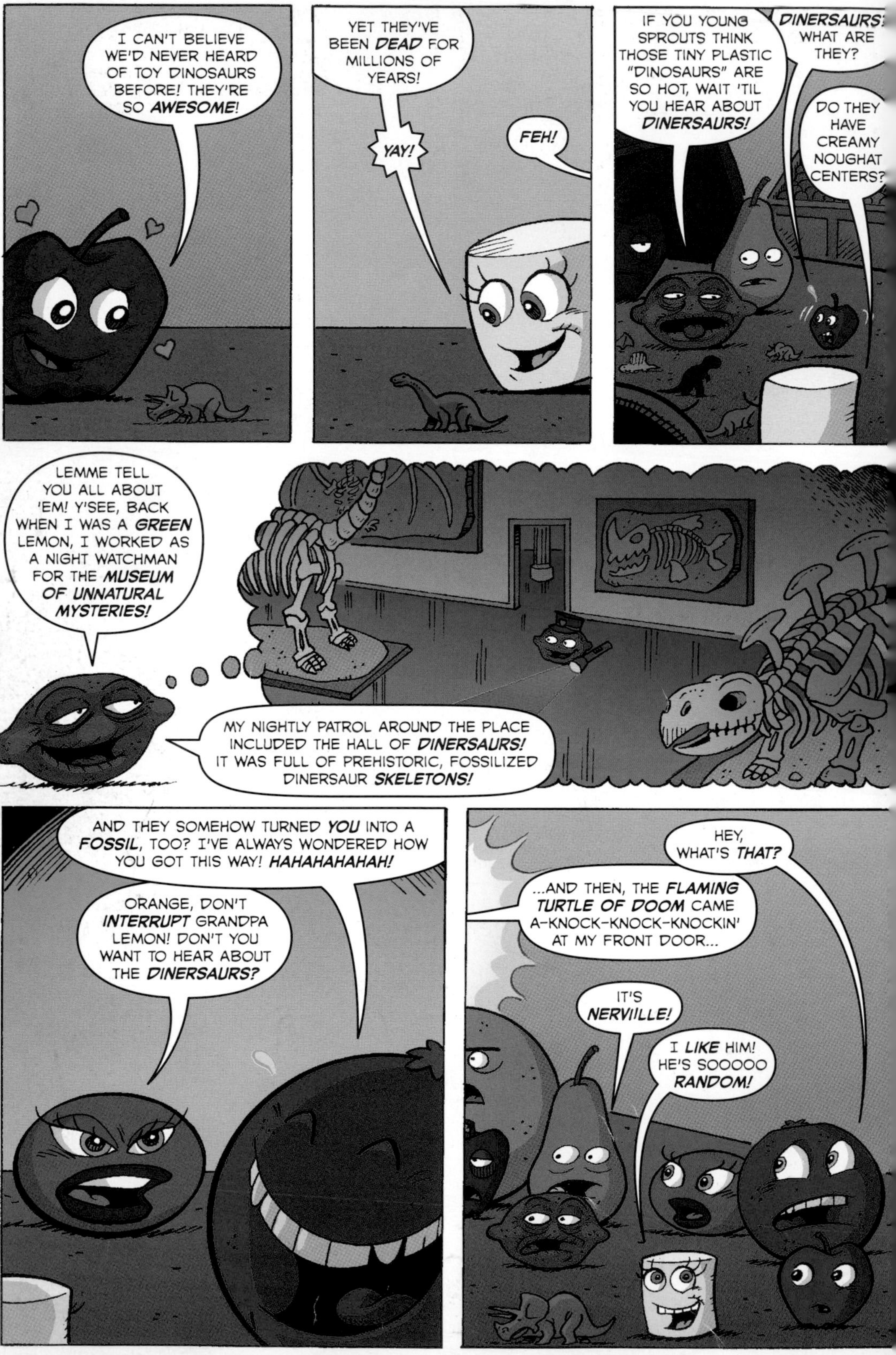
I CAN'T BELIEVE WE'D NEVER HEARD OF TOY DINOSAURS BEFORE! THEY'RE SO AWESOME!
YET THEY'VE BEEN DEAD FOR MILLIONS OF YEARS!
YAY!
FEH!
IF YOU YOUNG SPROUTS THINK THOSE TINY PLASTIC "DINOSAURS" ARE SO HOT, WAIT 'TIL YOU HEAR ABOUT DINERSAURS!
DINERSAURS? WHAT ARE THEY?
DO THEY HAVE CREAMY NOUGHAT CENTERS?
LEMME TELL YOU ALL ABOUT 'EM! Y'SEE, BACK WHEN I WAS A GREEN LEMON, I WORKED AS A NIGHT WATCHMAN FOR THE MUSEUM OF UNNATURAL MYSTERIES!
MY NIGHTLY PATROL AROUND THE PLACE INCLUDED THE HALL OF DINERSAURS! IT WAS FULL OF PREHISTORIC, FOSSILIZED DINERSAUR SKELETONS!
AND THEY SOMEHOW TURNED YOU INTO A FOSSIL, TOO? I'VE ALWAYS WONDERED HOW YOU GOT THIS WAY! HAHAHAHAHAH!
ORANGE, DON'T INTERRUPT GRANDPA LEMON! DON'T YOU WANT TO HEAR ABOUT THE DINERSAURS?
HEY, WHAT'S THAT?
...AND THEN, THE FLAMING TURTLE OF DOOM CAME A-KNOCK-KNOCK-KNOCKIN' AT MY FRONT DOOR...
IT'S NERVIILLE!
I LIKE HIM! HE'S SOOOOO RANDOM!

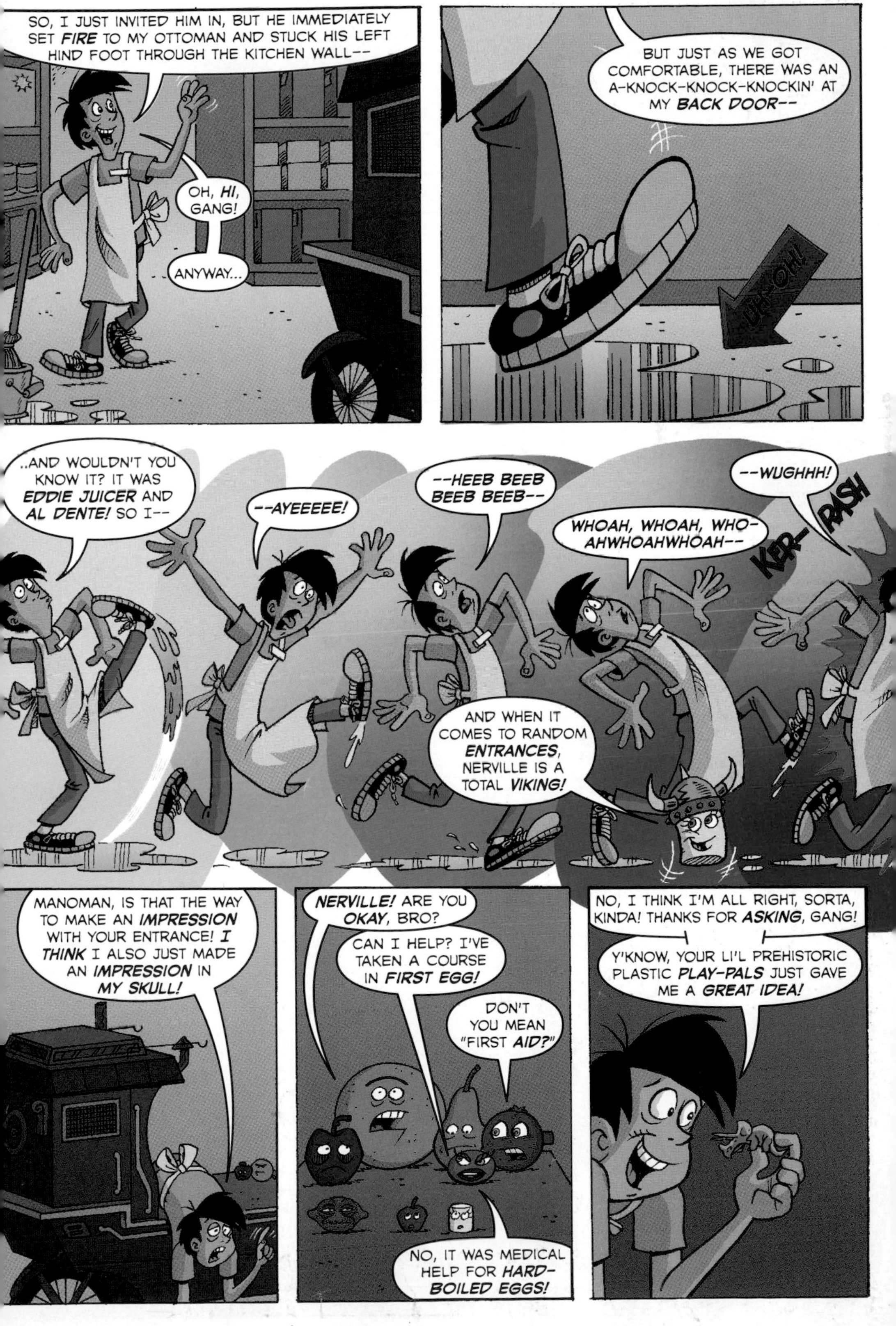
SO, I JUST INVITED HIM IN, BUT HE IMMEDIATELY SET FIRE TO MY OTTOMAN AND STUCK HIS LEFT HIND FOOT THROUGH THE KITCHEN WALL--
OH, HI, GANG!
ANYWAY...
BUT JUST AS WE GOT COMFORTABLE, THERE WAS AN A-KNOCK-KNOCK-KNOCKIN' AT MY BACK DOOR--
UH-OH!
..AND WOULDN'T YOU KNOW IT? IT WAS EDDIE JUICER AND AL DENTE! SO I--
--AYEEEEE!
--HEEB BEEB BEEB BEEB--
WHOAH, WHOAH, WHO-AHWHOAHWHOAH--
--WUGHHH!
KER-RASH
AND WHEN IT COMES TO RANDOM ENTRANCES, NERVILLE IS A TOTAL VIKING!
MANOMAN, IS THAT THE WAY TO MAKE AN IMPRESSION WITH YOUR ENTRANCE! I THINK I ALSO JUST MADE AN IMPRESSION IN MY SKULL!
NERVILLE! ARE YOU OKAY, BRO?
CAN I HELP? I'VE TAKEN A COURSE IN FIRST EGG!
DON'T YOU MEAN "FIRST AID?"
NO, IT WAS MEDICAL HELP FOR HARD-BOILED EGGS!
NO, I THINK I'M ALL RIGHT, SORTA, KINDA! THANKS FOR ASKING, GANG!
Y'KNOW, YOUR LI'L PREHISTORIC PLASTIC PLAY-PALS JUST GAVE ME A GREAT IDEA!

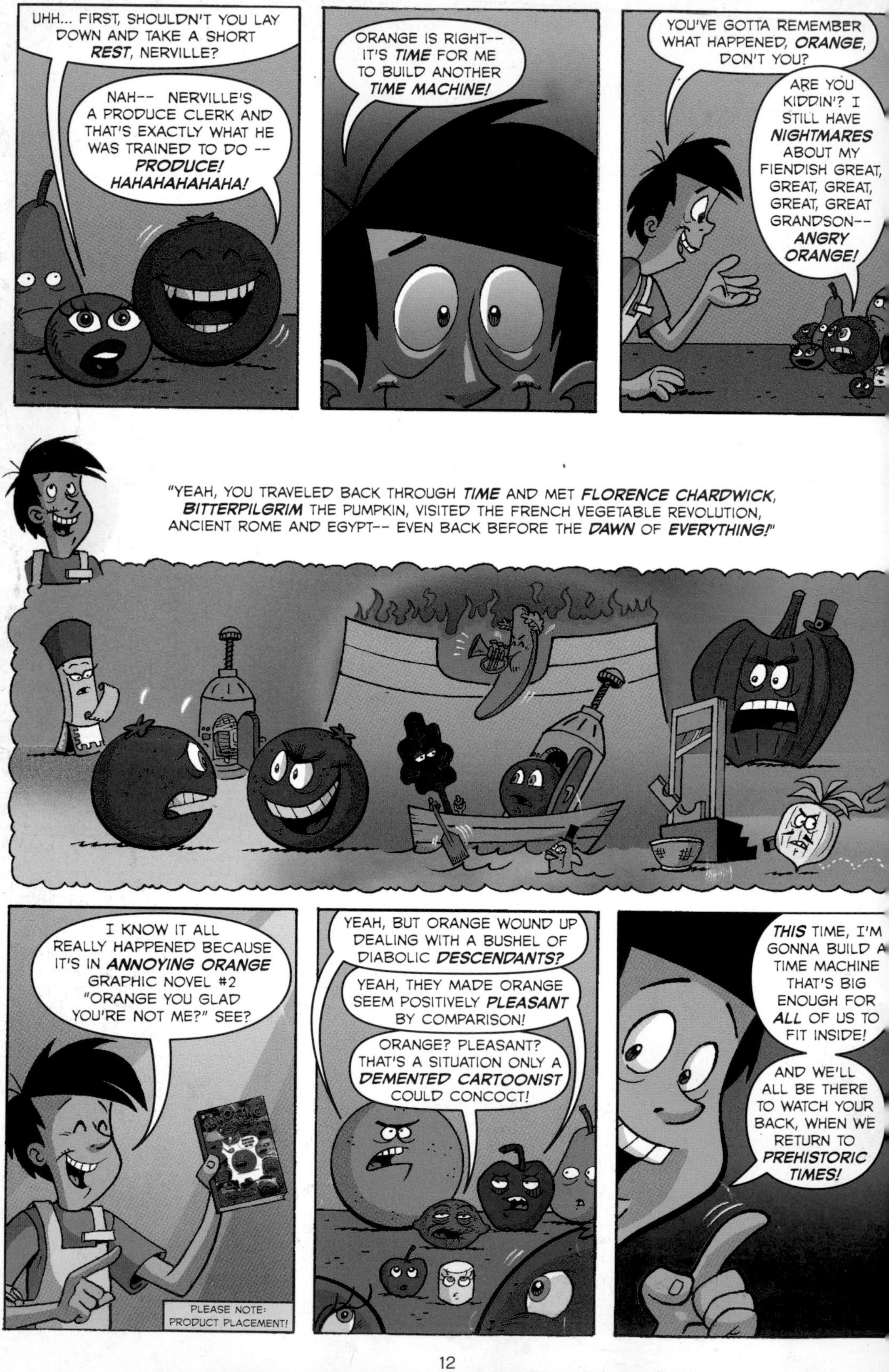
UHH... FIRST, SHOULDN'T YOU LAY DOWN AND TAKE A SHORT REST, NERVILLE?
NAH-- NERVILLE'S A PRODUCE CLERK AND THAT'S EXACTLY WHAT HE WAS TRAINED TO DO -- PRODUCE! HAHAHAHAHAHA!
ORANGE IS RIGHT-- IT'S TIME FOR ME TO BUILD ANOTHER TIME MACHINE!
YOU'VE GOTTA REMEMBER WHAT HAPPENED, ORANGE, DON'T YOU?
ARE YOU KIDDIN'? I STILL HAVE NIGHTMARES ABOUT MY FIENDISH GREAT, GREAT, GREAT, GREAT, GREAT GRANDSON-- ANGRY ORANGE!
"YEAH, YOU TRAVELED BACK THROUGH TIME AND MET FLORENCE CHARDWICK, BITTERPILGRIM THE PUMPKIN, VISITED THE FRENCH VEGETABLE REVOLUTION, ANCIENT ROME AND EGYPT-- EVEN BACK BEFORE THE DAWN OF EVERYTHING!"
I KNOW IT ALL REALLY HAPPENED BECAUSE IT'S IN ANNOYING ORANGE GRAPHIC NOVEL #2 "ORANGE YOU GLAD YOU'RE NOT ME?" SEE?
PLEASE NOTE: PRODUCT PLACEMENT!
YEAH, BUT ORANGE WOUND UP DEALING WITH A BUSHEL OF DIABOLIC DESCENDANTS?
YEAH, THEY MADE ORANGE SEEM POSITIVELY PLEASANT BY COMPARISON!
ORANGE? PLEASANT? THAT'S A SITUATION ONLY A DEMENTED CARTOONIST COULD CONCOCT!
THIS TIME, I'M GONNA BUILD A TIME MACHINE THAT'S BIG ENOUGH FOR ALL OF US TO FIT INSIDE!
AND WE'LL ALL BE THERE TO WATCH YOUR BACK, WHEN WE RETURN TO PREHISTORIC TIMES!

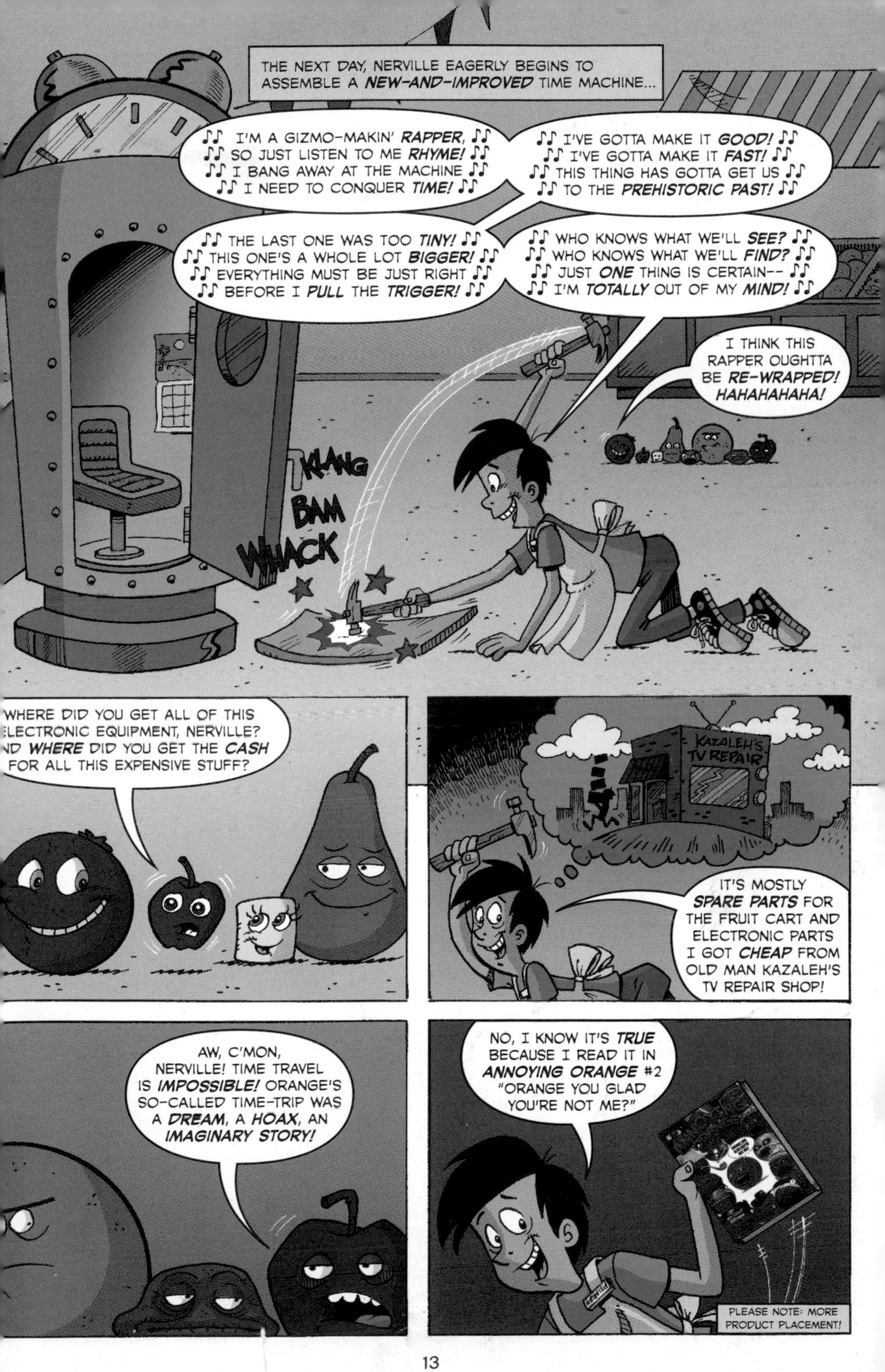

THE NEXT DAY, NERVILLE EAGERLY BEGINS TO ASSEMBLE A NEW-AND-IMPROVED TIME MACHINE...
♫ I'M A GIZMO-MAKIN' RAPPER, ♫ ♫ SO JUST LISTEN TO ME RHYME! ♫ ♫ I BANG AWAY AT THE MACHINE ♫ ♫ I NEED TO CONQUER TIME! ♫
♫ I'VE GOTTA MAKE IT GOOD! ♫ ♫ I'VE GOTTA MAKE IT FAST! ♫ ♫ THIS THING HAS GOTTA GET US ♫ ♫ TO THE PREHISTORIC PAST! ♫
♫ THE LAST ONE WAS TOO TINY! ♫ ♫ THIS ONE'S A WHOLE LOT BIGGER! ♫ ♫ EVERYTHING MUST BE JUST RIGHT ♫ ♫ BEFORE I PULL THE TRIGGER! ♫
♫ WHO KNOWS WHAT WE'LL SEE? ♫ ♫ WHO KNOWS WHAT WE'LL FIND? ♫ ♫ JUST ONE THING IS CERTAIN-- ♫ ♫ I'M TOTALLY OUT OF MY MIND! ♫
I THINK THIS RAPPER OUGHTTA BE RE-WRAPPED! HAHAHAHAHA!
KLANG
BAM
WHACK
WHERE DID YOU GET ALL OF THIS ELECTRONIC EQUIPMENT, NERVILLE? AND WHERE DID YOU GET THE CASH FOR ALL THIS EXPENSIVE STUFF?
KAZALEH'S TV REPAIR
IT'S MOSTLY SPARE PARTS FOR THE FRUIT CART AND ELECTRONIC PARTS I GOT CHEAP FROM OLD MAN KAZALEH'S TV REPAIR SHOP!
AW, C'MON, NERVILLE! TIME TRAVEL IS IMPOSSIBLE! ORANGE'S SO-CALLED TIME-TRIP WAS A DREAM, A HOAX, AN IMAGINARY STORY!
NO, I KNOW IT'S TRUE BECAUSE I READ IT IN ANNOYING ORANGE #2 "ORANGE YOU GLAD YOU'RE NOT ME?"
PLEASE NOTE: MORE PRODUCT PLACEMENT!

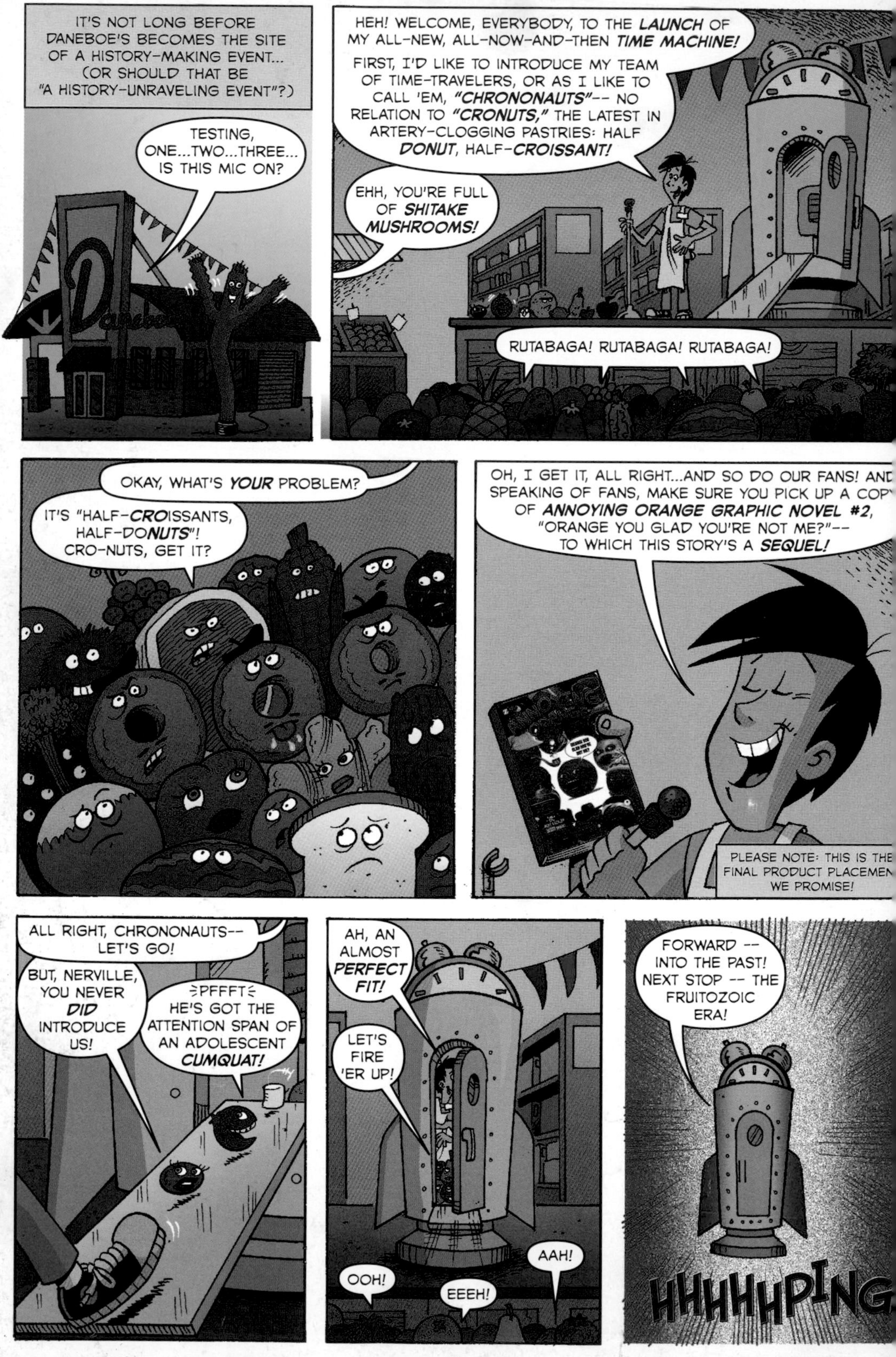

IT'S NOT LONG BEFORE DANEBOE'S BECOMES THE SITE OF A HISTORY-MAKING EVENT... (OR SHOULD THAT BE "A HISTORY-UNRAVELING EVENT"?)
TESTING, ONE...TWO...THREE... IS THIS MIC ON?
HEH! WELCOME, EVERYBODY, TO THE LAUNCH OF MY ALL-NEW, ALL-NOW-AND-THEN TIME MACHINE!
FIRST, I'D LIKE TO INTRODUCE MY TEAM OF TIME-TRAVELERS, OR AS I LIKE TO CALL 'EM, "CHRONONAUTS"-- NO RELATION TO "CRONUTS," THE LATEST IN ARTERY-CLOGGING PASTRIES: HALF DONUT, HALF-CROISSANT!
EHH, YOU'RE FULL OF SHITAKE MUSHROOMS!
RUTABAGA! RUTABAGA! RUTABAGA!
OKAY, WHAT'S YOUR PROBLEM?
IT'S "HALF-CROISSANTS, HALF-DONUTS"! CRO-NUTS, GET IT?
OH, I GET IT, ALL RIGHT...AND SO DO OUR FANS! AND SPEAKING OF FANS, MAKE SURE YOU PICK UP A COPY OF ANNOYING ORANGE GRAPHIC NOVEL #2, "ORANGE YOU GLAD YOU'RE NOT ME?"-- TO WHICH THIS STORY'S A SEQUEL!
PLEASE NOTE: THIS IS THE FINAL PRODUCT PLACEMENT WE PROMISE!
ALL RIGHT, CHRONONAUTS-- LET'S GO!
BUT, NERVILLE, YOU NEVER DID INTRODUCE US!
PFFFT HE'S GOT THE ATTENTION SPAN OF AN ADOLESCENT CUMQUAT!
AH, AN ALMOST PERFECT FIT!
LET'S FIRE 'ER UP!
OOH!
EEEH!
AAH!
FORWARD -- INTO THE PAST! NEXT STOP -- THE FRUITOZOIC ERA!
HHHHHPING

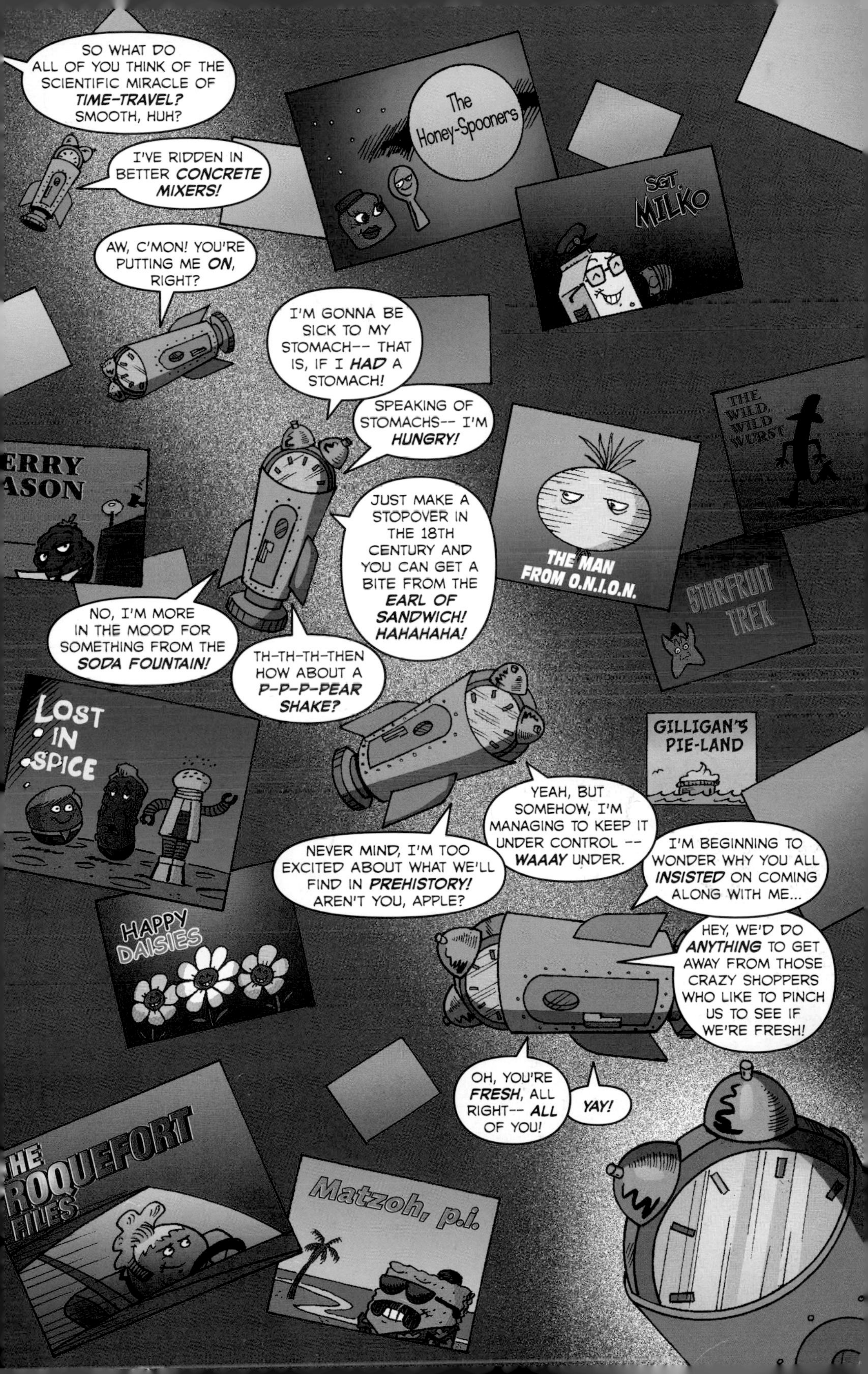
SO WHAT DO ALL OF YOU THINK OF THE SCIENTIFIC MIRACLE OF TIME-TRAVEL? SMOOTH, HUH?
I'VE RIDDEN IN BETTER CONCRETE MIXERS!
AW, C'MON! YOU'RE PUTTING ME ON, RIGHT?
I'M GONNA BE SICK TO MY STOMACH-- THAT IS, IF I HAD A STOMACH!
SPEAKING OF STOMACHS-- I'M HUNGRY!
JUST MAKE A STOPOVER IN THE 18TH CENTURY AND YOU CAN GET A BITE FROM THE EARL OF SANDWICH! HAHAHAHA!
NO, I'M MORE IN THE MOOD FOR SOMETHING FROM THE SODA FOUNTAIN!
TH-TH-TH-THEN HOW ABOUT A P-P-P-PEAR SHAKE?
NEVER MIND, I'M TOO EXCITED ABOUT WHAT WE'LL FIND IN PREHISTORY! AREN'T YOU, APPLE?
YEAH, BUT SOMEHOW, I'M MANAGING TO KEEP IT UNDER CONTROL -- WAAAY UNDER.
I'M BEGINNING TO WONDER WHY YOU ALL INSISTED ON COMING ALONG WITH ME...
HEY, WE'D DO ANYTHING TO GET AWAY FROM THOSE CRAZY SHOPPERS WHO LIKE TO PINCH US TO SEE IF WE'RE FRESH!
OH, YOU'RE FRESH, ALL RIGHT-- ALL OF YOU!
YAY!
The Honey-Spooners
SGT. MILKO
ERRY
ASON
THE WILD, WILD WURST
THE MAN FROM O.N.I.O.N.
STARFRUIT TREK
LOST IN SPICE
GILLIGAN'S PIE-LAND
HAPPY DAISIES
THE ROQUEFORT FILES
Matzoh, p.i.

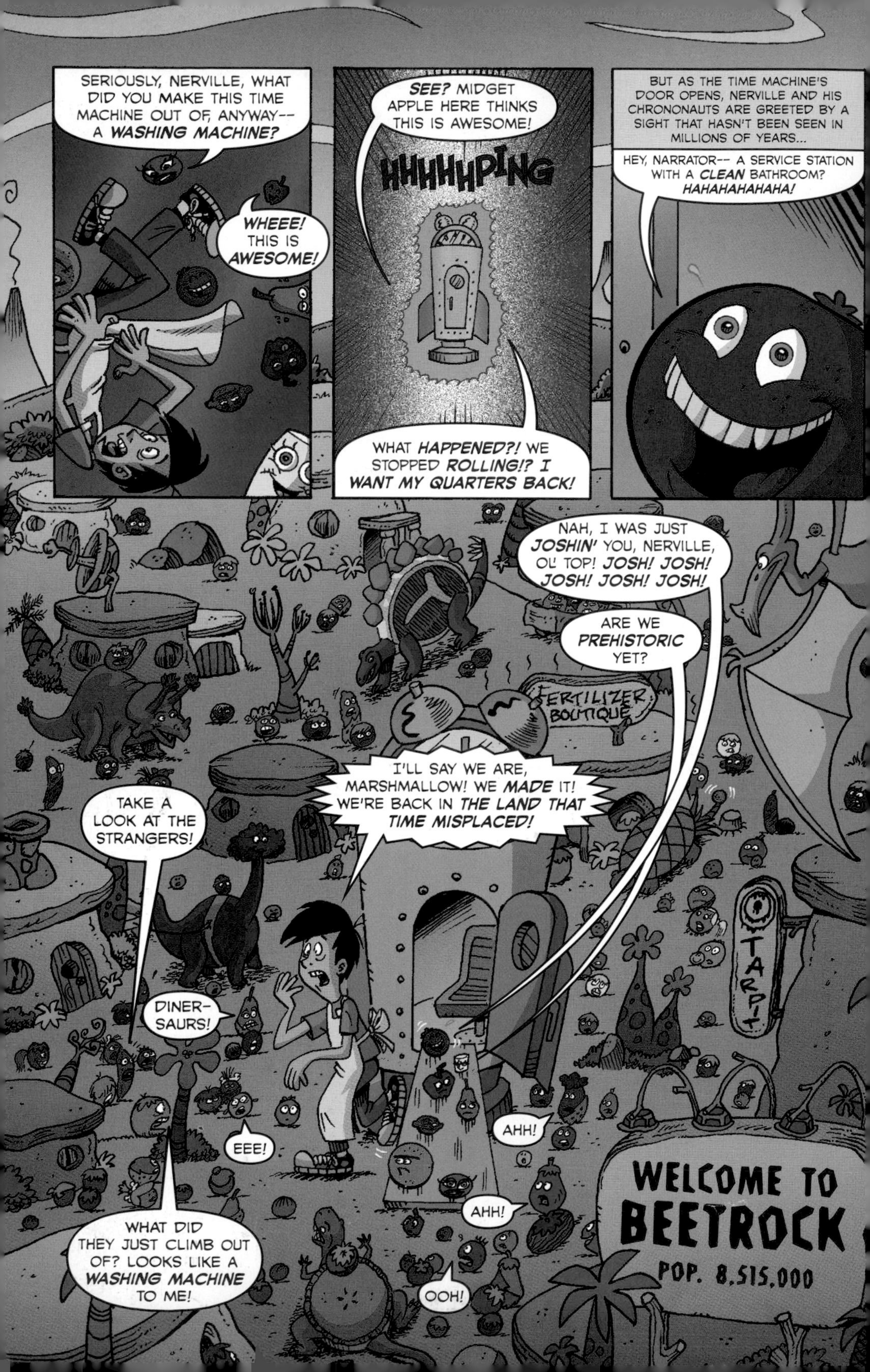
SERIOUSLY, NERVILLE, WHAT DID YOU MAKE THIS TIME MACHINE OUT OF, ANYWAY-- A WASHING MACHINE?
WHEEE! THIS IS AWESOME!
SEE? MIDGET APPLE HERE THINKS THIS IS AWESOME!
HHHHHPING
WHAT HAPPENED?! WE STOPPED ROLLING!? I WANT MY QUARTERS BACK!
BUT AS THE TIME MACHINE'S DOOR OPENS, NERVILLE AND HIS CHRONONAUTS ARE GREETED BY A SIGHT THAT HASN'T BEEN SEEN IN MILLIONS OF YEARS...
HEY, NARRATOR-- A SERVICE STATION WITH A CLEAN BATHROOM? HAHAHAHAHAHA!
NAH, I WAS JUST JOSHIN' YOU, NERVILLE, OL' TOP! JOSH! JOSH! JOSH! JOSH! JOSH!
ARE WE PREHISTORIC YET?
FERTILIZER BOUTIQUE
I'LL SAY WE ARE, MARSHMALLOW! WE MADE IT! WE'RE BACK IN THE LAND THAT TIME MISPLACED!
TAKE A LOOK AT THE STRANGERS!
DINER-SAURS!
TARPIT
EEE!
AHH!
AHH!
WHAT DID THEY JUST CLIMB OUT OF? LOOKS LIKE A WASHING MACHINE TO ME!
OOH!
WELCOME TO BEETROCK
POP. 8,515,000

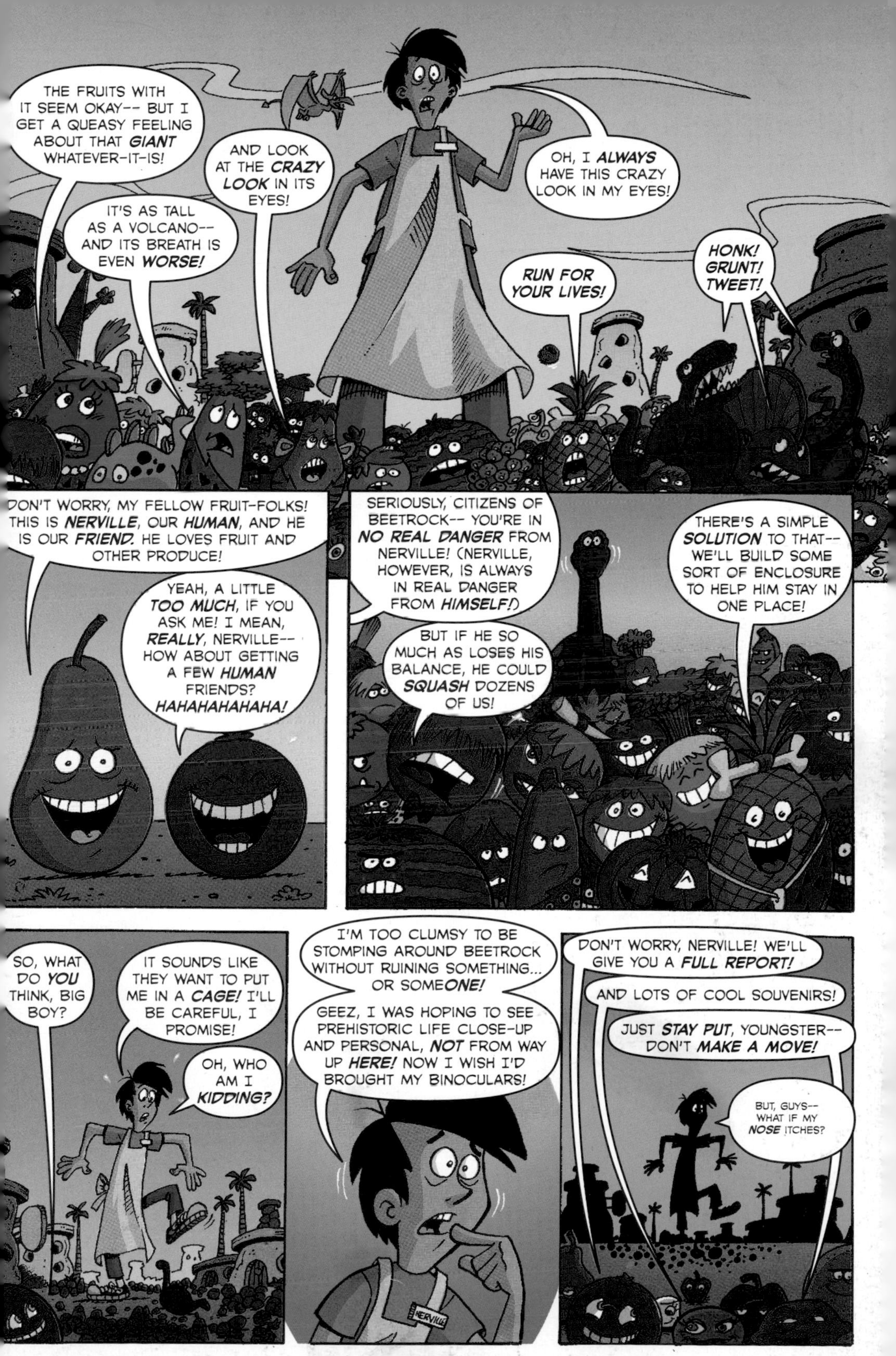
THE FRUITS WITH IT SEEM OKAY-- BUT I GET A QUEASY FEELING ABOUT THAT GIANT WHATEVER-IT-IS!
IT'S AS TALL AS A VOLCANO-- AND ITS BREATH IS EVEN WORSE!
AND LOOK AT THE CRAZY LOOK IN ITS EYES!
OH, I ALWAYS HAVE THIS CRAZY LOOK IN MY EYES!
RUN FOR YOUR LIVES!
HONK! GRUNT! TWEET!
DON'T WORRY, MY FELLOW FRUIT-FOLKS! THIS IS NERVILLE, OUR HUMAN, AND HE IS OUR FRIEND. HE LOVES FRUIT AND OTHER PRODUCE!
YEAH, A LITTLE TOO MUCH, IF YOU ASK ME! I MEAN, REALLY, NERVILLE-- HOW ABOUT GETTING A FEW HUMAN FRIENDS? HAHAHAHAHAHA!
SERIOUSLY, CITIZENS OF BEETROCK-- YOU'RE IN NO REAL DANGER FROM NERVILLE! (NERVILLE, HOWEVER, IS ALWAYS IN REAL DANGER FROM HIMSELF!)
BUT IF HE SO MUCH AS LOSES HIS BALANCE, HE COULD SQUASH DOZENS OF US!
THERE'S A SIMPLE SOLUTION TO THAT-- WE'LL BUILD SOME SORT OF ENCLOSURE TO HELP HIM STAY IN ONE PLACE!
SO, WHAT DO YOU THINK, BIG BOY?
IT SOUNDS LIKE THEY WANT TO PUT ME IN A CAGE! I'LL BE CAREFUL, I PROMISE!
OH, WHO AM I KIDDING?
I'M TOO CLUMSY TO BE STOMPING AROUND BEETROCK WITHOUT RUINING SOMETHING... OR SOMEONE!
GEEZ, I WAS HOPING TO SEE PREHISTORIC LIFE CLOSE-UP AND PERSONAL, NOT FROM WAY UP HERE! NOW I WISH I'D BROUGHT MY BINOCULARS!
NERVILLE
DON'T WORRY, NERVILLE! WE'LL GIVE YOU A FULL REPORT!
AND LOTS OF COOL SOUVENIRS!
JUST STAY PUT, YOUNGSTER-- DON'T MAKE A MOVE!
BUT, GUYS-- WHAT IF MY NOSE ITCHES?

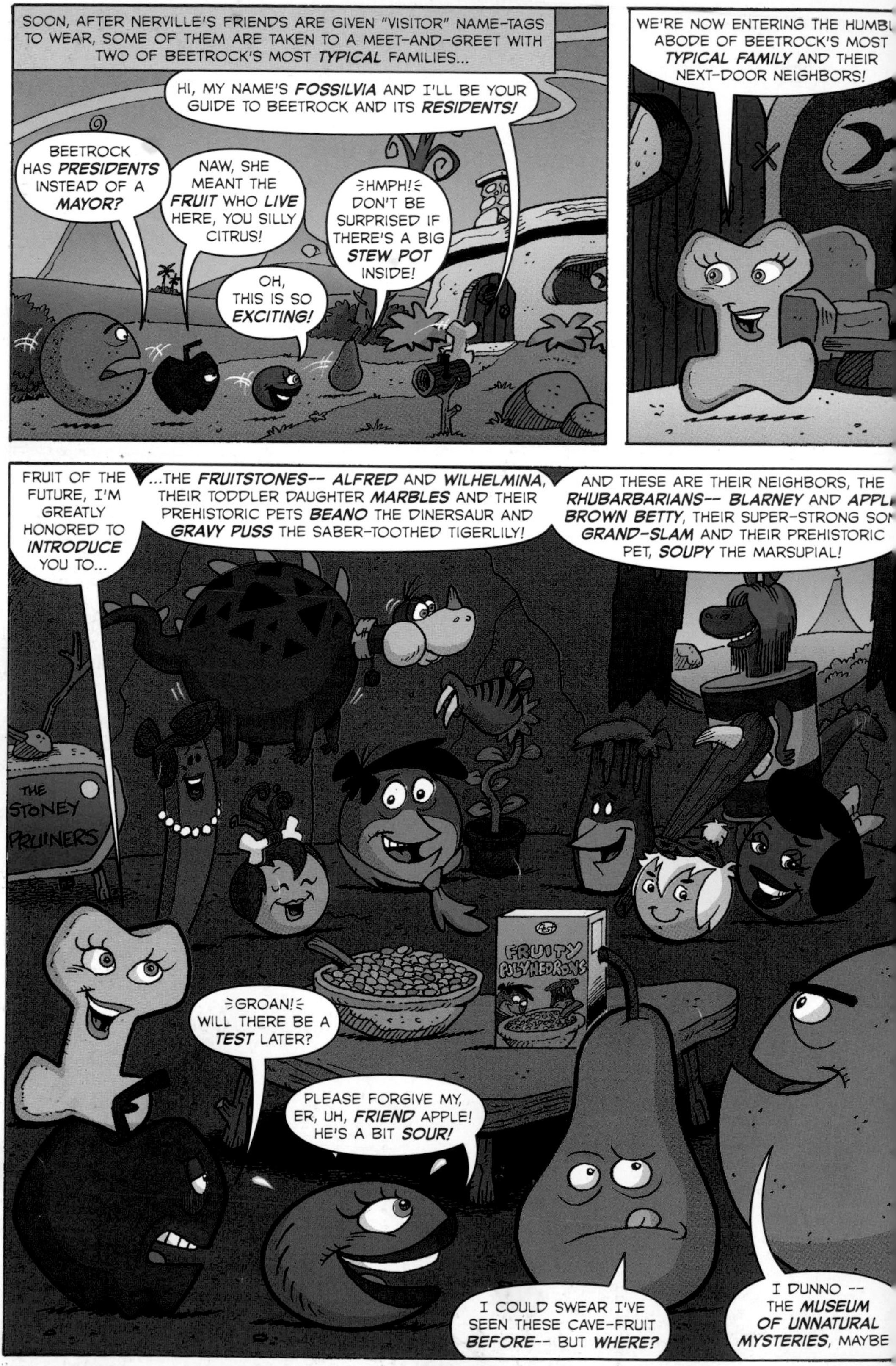
SOON, AFTER NERVILLE'S FRIENDS ARE GIVEN "VISITOR" NAME-TAGS TO WEAR, SOME OF THEM ARE TAKEN TO A MEET-AND-GREET WITH TWO OF BEETROCK'S MOST TYPICAL FAMILIES...
HI, MY NAME'S FOSSILVIA AND I'LL BE YOUR GUIDE TO BEETROCK AND ITS RESIDENTS!
BEETROCK HAS PRESIDENTS INSTEAD OF A MAYOR?
NAW, SHE MEANT THE FRUIT WHO LIVE HERE, YOU SILLY CITRUS!
OH, THIS IS SO EXCITING!
HMPH! DON'T BE SURPRISED IF THERE'S A BIG STEW POT INSIDE!
WE'RE NOW ENTERING THE HUMBL ABODE OF BEETROCK'S MOST TYPICAL FAMILY AND THEIR NEXT-DOOR NEIGHBORS!
FRUIT OF THE FUTURE, I'M GREATLY HONORED TO INTRODUCE YOU TO...
...THE FRUITSTONES-- ALFRED AND WILHELMINA, THEIR TODDLER DAUGHTER MARBLES AND THEIR PREHISTORIC PETS BEANO THE DINERSAUR AND GRAVY PUSS THE SABER-TOOTHED TIGERLILY!
AND THESE ARE THEIR NEIGHBORS, THE RHUBARBARIANS-- BLARNEY AND APPL BROWN BETTY, THEIR SUPER-STRONG SON GRAND-SLAM AND THEIR PREHISTORIC PET, SOUPY THE MARSUPIAL!
THE STONEY PRUINERS
FRUITY POLYHEDRONS
GROAN! WILL THERE BE A TEST LATER?
PLEASE FORGIVE MY, ER, UH, FRIEND APPLE! HE'S A BIT SOUR!
I COULD SWEAR I'VE SEEN THESE CAVE-FRUIT BEFORE-- BUT WHERE?
I DUNNO -- THE MUSEUM OF UNNATURAL MYSTERIES, MAYBE

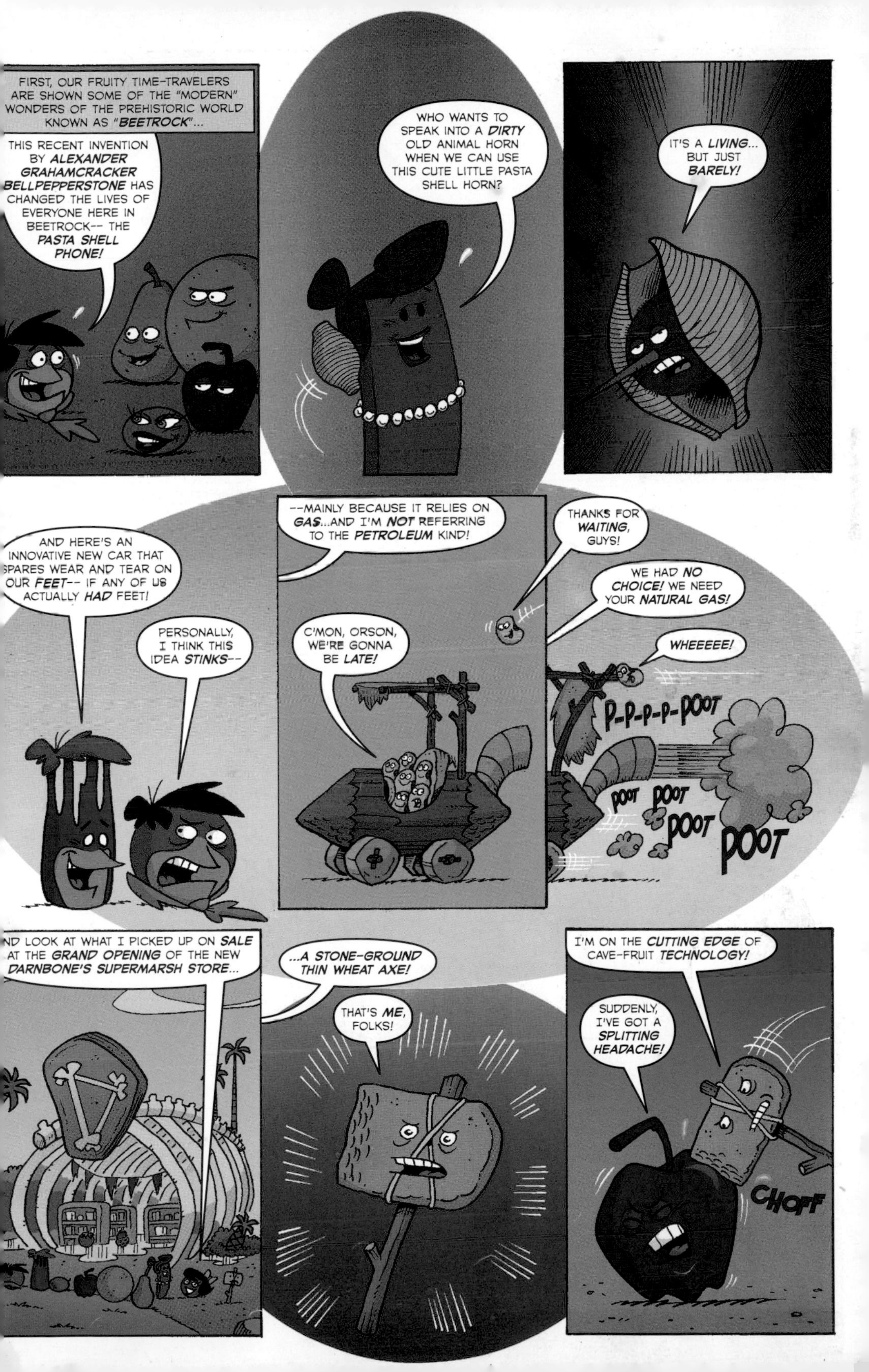
FIRST, OUR FRUITY TIME-TRAVELERS ARE SHOWN SOME OF THE "MODERN" WONDERS OF THE PREHISTORIC WORLD KNOWN AS "BEETROCK"...
THIS RECENT INVENTION BY ALEXANDER GRAHAMCRACKER BELLPEPPERSTONE HAS CHANGED THE LIVES OF EVERYONE HERE IN BEETROCK-- THE PASTA SHELL PHONE!
WHO WANTS TO SPEAK INTO A DIRTY OLD ANIMAL HORN WHEN WE CAN USE THIS CUTE LITTLE PASTA SHELL HORN?
IT'S A LIVING... BUT JUST BARELY!
AND HERE'S AN INNOVATIVE NEW CAR THAT SPARES WEAR AND TEAR ON OUR FEET-- IF ANY OF US ACTUALLY HAD FEET!
PERSONALLY, I THINK THIS IDEA STINKS--
--MAINLY BECAUSE IT RELIES ON GAS...AND I'M NOT REFERRING TO THE PETROLEUM KIND!
C'MON, ORSON, WE'RE GONNA BE LATE!
THANKS FOR WAITING, GUYS!
WE HAD NO CHOICE! WE NEED YOUR NATURAL GAS!
WHEEEEE!
P-P-P-P-POOT
POOT POOT POOT POOT
ND LOOK AT WHAT I PICKED UP ON SALE AT THE GRAND OPENING OF THE NEW DARNBONE'S SUPERMARSH STORE...
...A STONE-GROUND THIN WHEAT AXE!
THAT'S ME, FOLKS!
I'M ON THE CUTTING EDGE OF CAVE-FRUIT TECHNOLOGY!
SUDDENLY, I'VE GOT A SPLITTING HEADACHE!
CHOFF

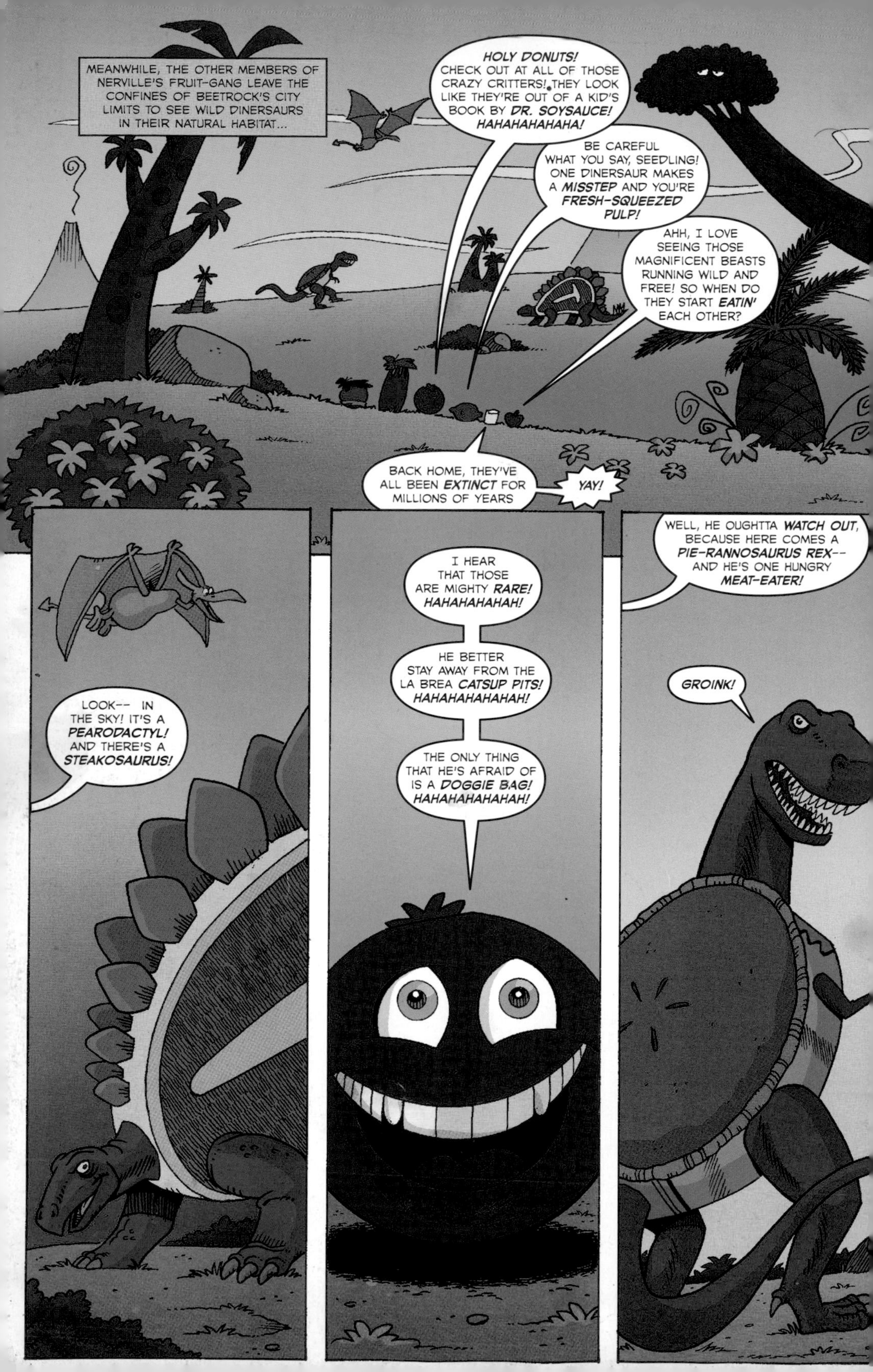
MEANWHILE, THE OTHER MEMBERS OF NERVILLE'S FRUIT-GANG LEAVE THE CONFINES OF BEETROCK'S CITY LIMITS TO SEE WILD DINERSAURS IN THEIR NATURAL HABITAT...
HOLY DONUTS! CHECK OUT AT ALL OF THOSE CRAZY CRITTERS! THEY LOOK LIKE THEY'RE OUT OF A KID'S BOOK BY DR. SOYSAUCE! HAHAHAHAHAHA!
BE CAREFUL WHAT YOU SAY, SEEDLING! ONE DINERSAUR MAKES A MISSTEP AND YOU'RE FRESH-SQUEEZED PULP!
AHH, I LOVE SEEING THOSE MAGNIFICENT BEASTS RUNNING WILD AND FREE! SO WHEN DO THEY START EATIN' EACH OTHER?
BACK HOME, THEY'VE ALL BEEN EXTINCT FOR MILLIONS OF YEARS
YAY!
LOOK-- IN THE SKY! IT'S A PEARODACTYL! AND THERE'S A STEAKOSAURUS!
I HEAR THAT THOSE ARE MIGHTY RARE! HAHAHAHAHAH!
HE BETTER STAY AWAY FROM THE LA BREA CATSUP PITS! HAHAHAHAHAHAH!
THE ONLY THING THAT HE'S AFRAID OF IS A DOGGIE BAG! HAHAHAHAHAHAH!
WELL, HE OUGHTTA WATCH OUT, BECAUSE HERE COMES A PIE-RANNOSAURUS REX-- AND HE'S ONE HUNGRY MEAT-EATER!
GROINK!

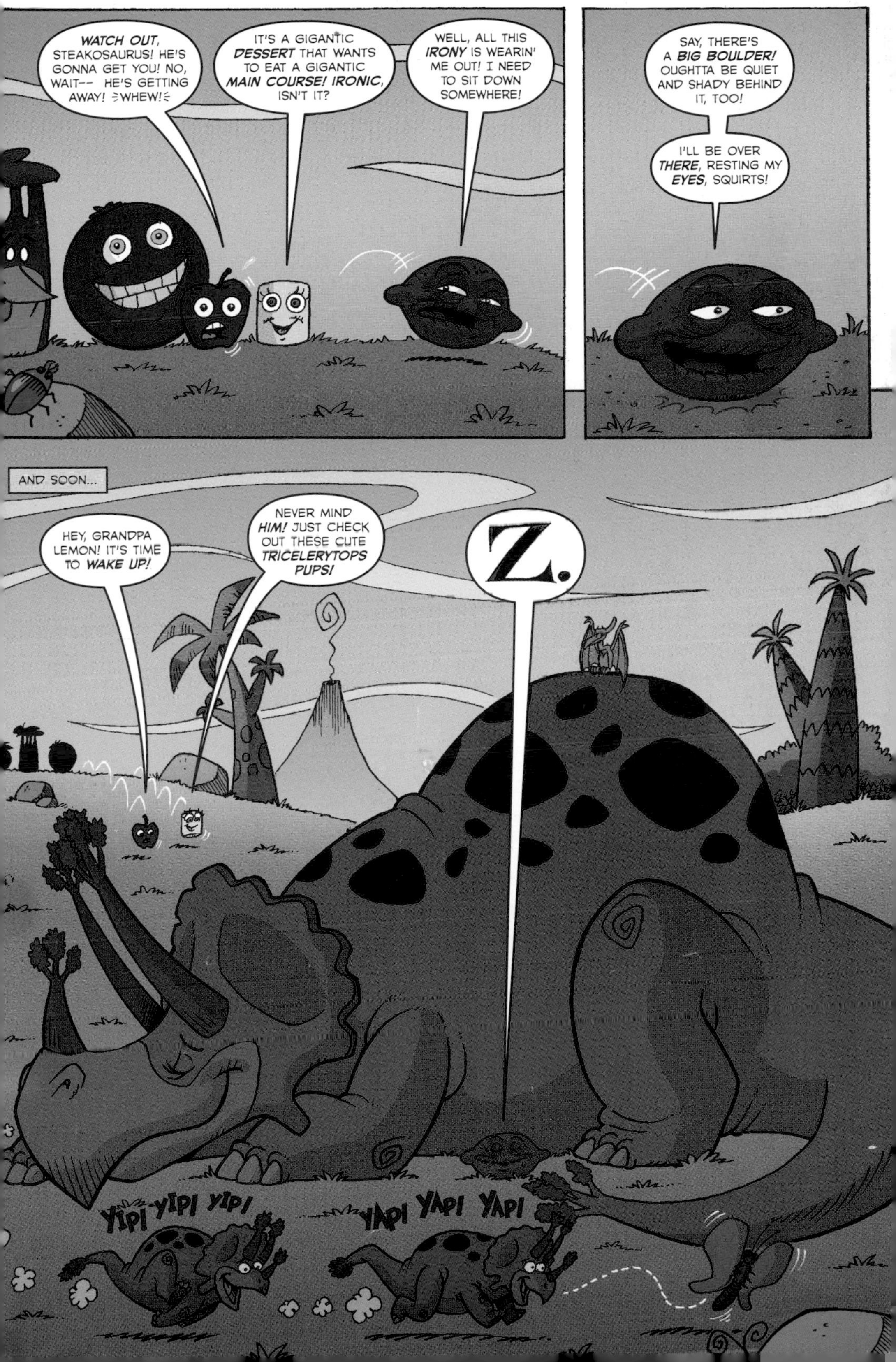
WATCH OUT, STEAKOSAURUS! HE'S GONNA GET YOU! NO, WAIT-- HE'S GETTING AWAY! WHEW!
IT'S A GIGANTIC DESSERT THAT WANTS TO EAT A GIGANTIC MAIN COURSE! IRONIC, ISN'T IT?
WELL, ALL THIS IRONY IS WEARIN' ME OUT! I NEED TO SIT DOWN SOMEWHERE!
SAY, THERE'S A BIG BOULDER! OUGHTTA BE QUIET AND SHADY BEHIND IT, TOO!
I'LL BE OVER THERE, RESTING MY EYES, SQUIRTS!
AND SOON...
HEY, GRANDPA LEMON! IT'S TIME TO WAKE UP!
NEVER MIND HIM! JUST CHECK OUT THESE CUTE TRICELERYTOPS PUPS!
Z.
YIP! YIP! YIP!
YAP! YAP! YAP!

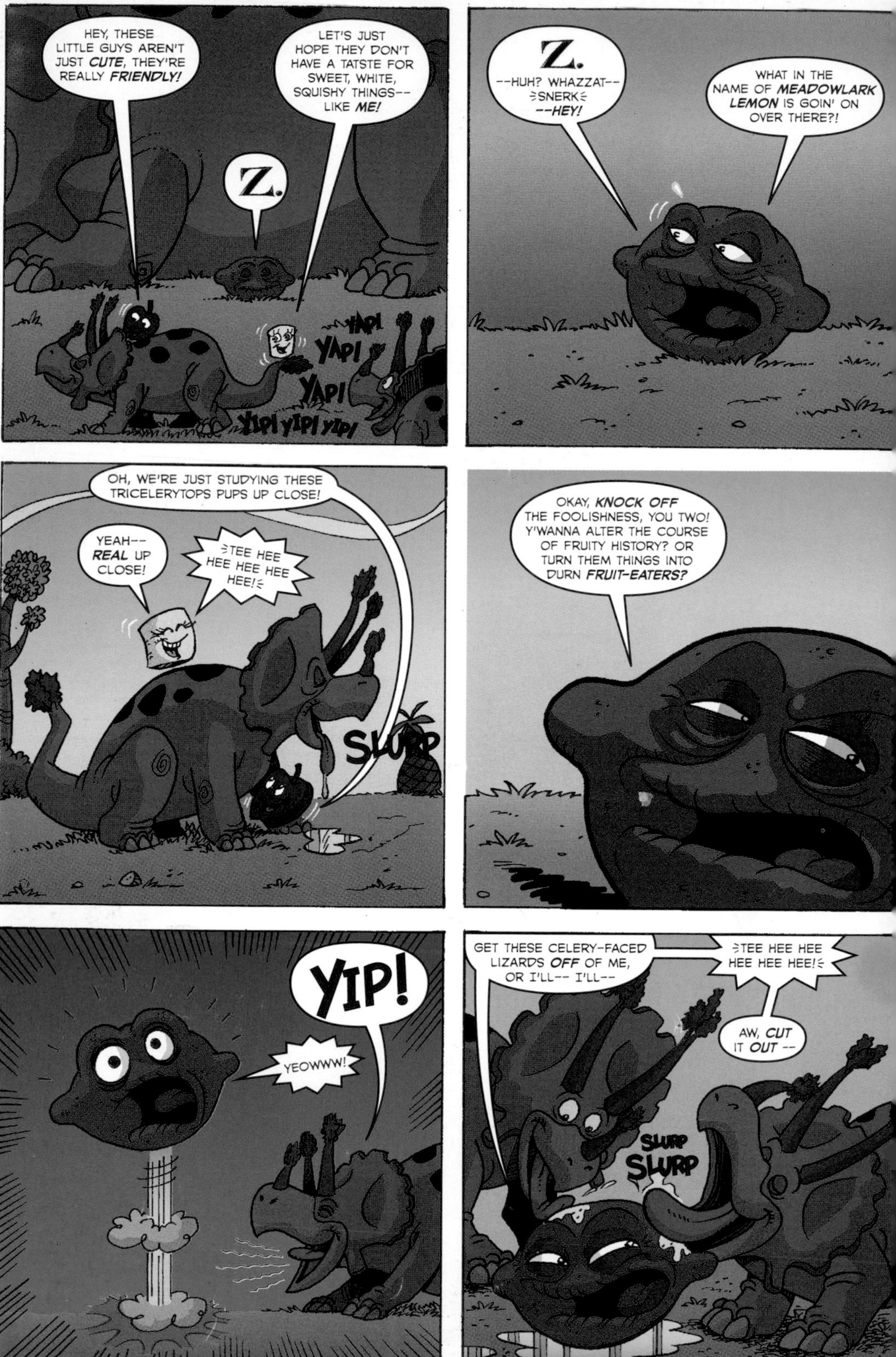
HEY, THESE LITTLE GUYS AREN'T JUST CUTE, THEY'RE REALLY FRIENDLY!
LET'S JUST HOPE THEY DON'T HAVE A TATSTE FOR SWEET, WHITE, SQUISHY THINGS-- LIKE ME!
Z.
YAP! YAP! YAP!
YIP! YIP! YIP!
Z.
--HUH? WHAZZAT-- ≷SNERK≶ --HEY!
WHAT IN THE NAME OF MEADOWLARK LEMON IS GOIN' ON OVER THERE?!
OH, WE'RE JUST STUDYING THESE TRICELERYTOPS PUPS UP CLOSE!
YEAH-- REAL UP CLOSE!
≷TEE HEE HEE HEE HEE HEE!≶
SLURP
OKAY, KNOCK OFF THE FOOLISHNESS, YOU TWO! Y'WANNA ALTER THE COURSE OF FRUITY HISTORY? OR TURN THEM THINGS INTO DURN FRUIT-EATERS?
YIP!
YEOWWW!
GET THESE CELERY-FACED LIZARDS OFF OF ME, OR I'LL-- I'LL--
≷TEE HEE HEE HEE HEE HEE!≶
AW, CUT IT OUT --
SLURP SLURP

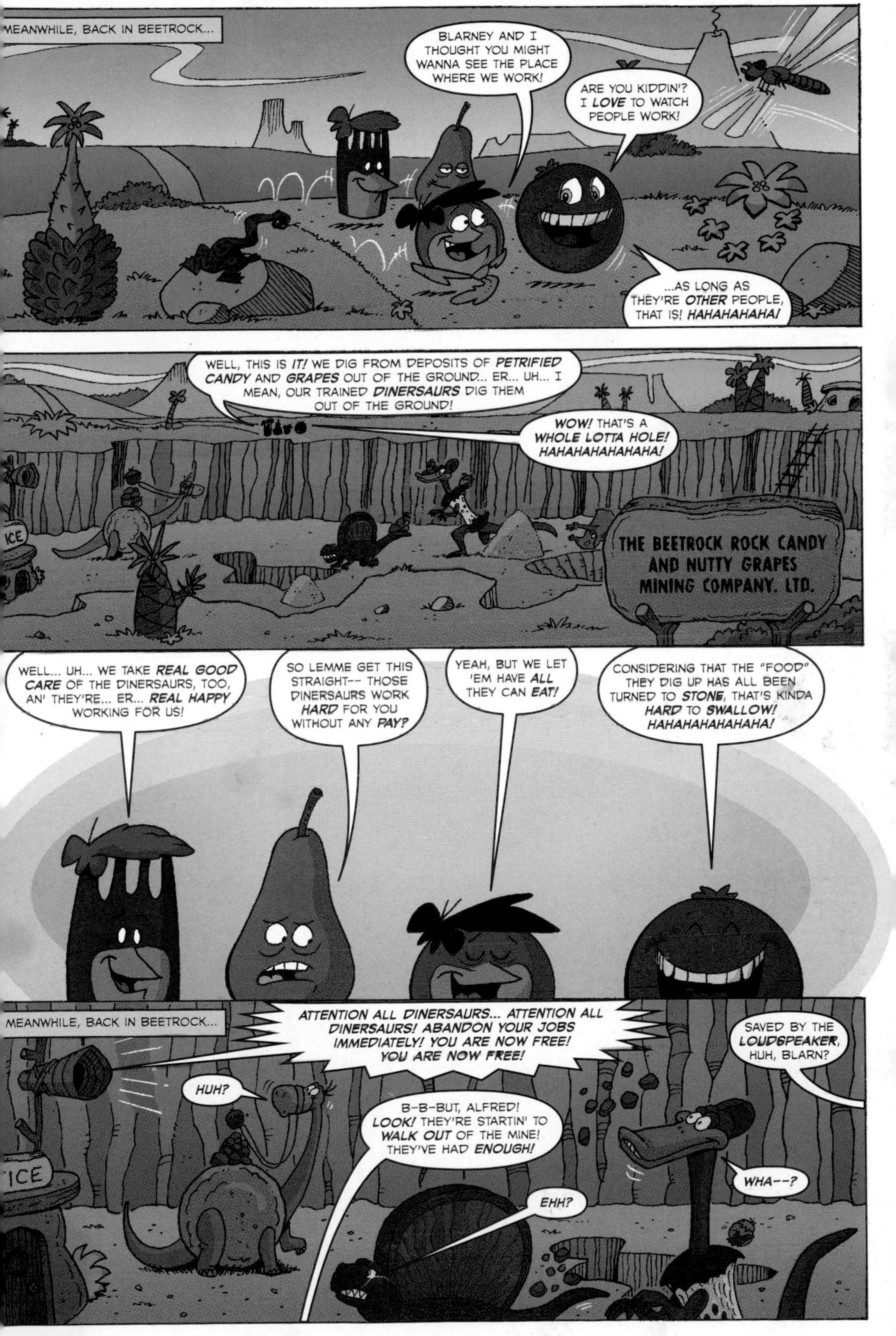
MEANWHILE, BACK IN BEETROCK...
BLARNEY AND I THOUGHT YOU MIGHT WANNA SEE THE PLACE WHERE WE WORK!
ARE YOU KIDDIN'? I LOVE TO WATCH PEOPLE WORK!
...AS LONG AS THEY'RE OTHER PEOPLE, THAT IS! HAHAHAHAHA!
WELL, THIS IS IT! WE DIG FROM DEPOSITS OF PETRIFIED CANDY AND GRAPES OUT OF THE GROUND... ER... UH... I MEAN, OUR TRAINED DINERSAURS DIG THEM OUT OF THE GROUND!
WOW! THAT'S A WHOLE LOTTA HOLE! HAHAHAHAHAHAHA!
THE BEETROCK ROCK CANDY AND NUTTY GRAPES MINING COMPANY. LTD.
WELL... UH... WE TAKE REAL GOOD CARE OF THE DINERSAURS, TOO, AN' THEY'RE... ER... REAL HAPPY WORKING FOR US!
SO LEMME GET THIS STRAIGHT-- THOSE DINERSAURS WORK HARD FOR YOU WITHOUT ANY PAY?
YEAH, BUT WE LET 'EM HAVE ALL THEY CAN EAT!
CONSIDERING THAT THE "FOOD" THEY DIG UP HAS ALL BEEN TURNED TO STONE, THAT'S KINDA HARD TO SWALLOW! HAHAHAHAHAHAHA!
MEANWHILE, BACK IN BEETROCK...
ATTENTION ALL DINERSAURS... ATTENTION ALL DINERSAURS! ABANDON YOUR JOBS IMMEDIATELY! YOU ARE NOW FREE! YOU ARE NOW FREE!
SAVED BY THE LOUDSPEAKER, HUH, BLARN?
HUH?
B-B-BUT, ALFRED! LOOK! THEY'RE STARTIN' TO WALK OUT OF THE MINE! THEY'VE HAD ENOUGH!
WHA--?
EHH?

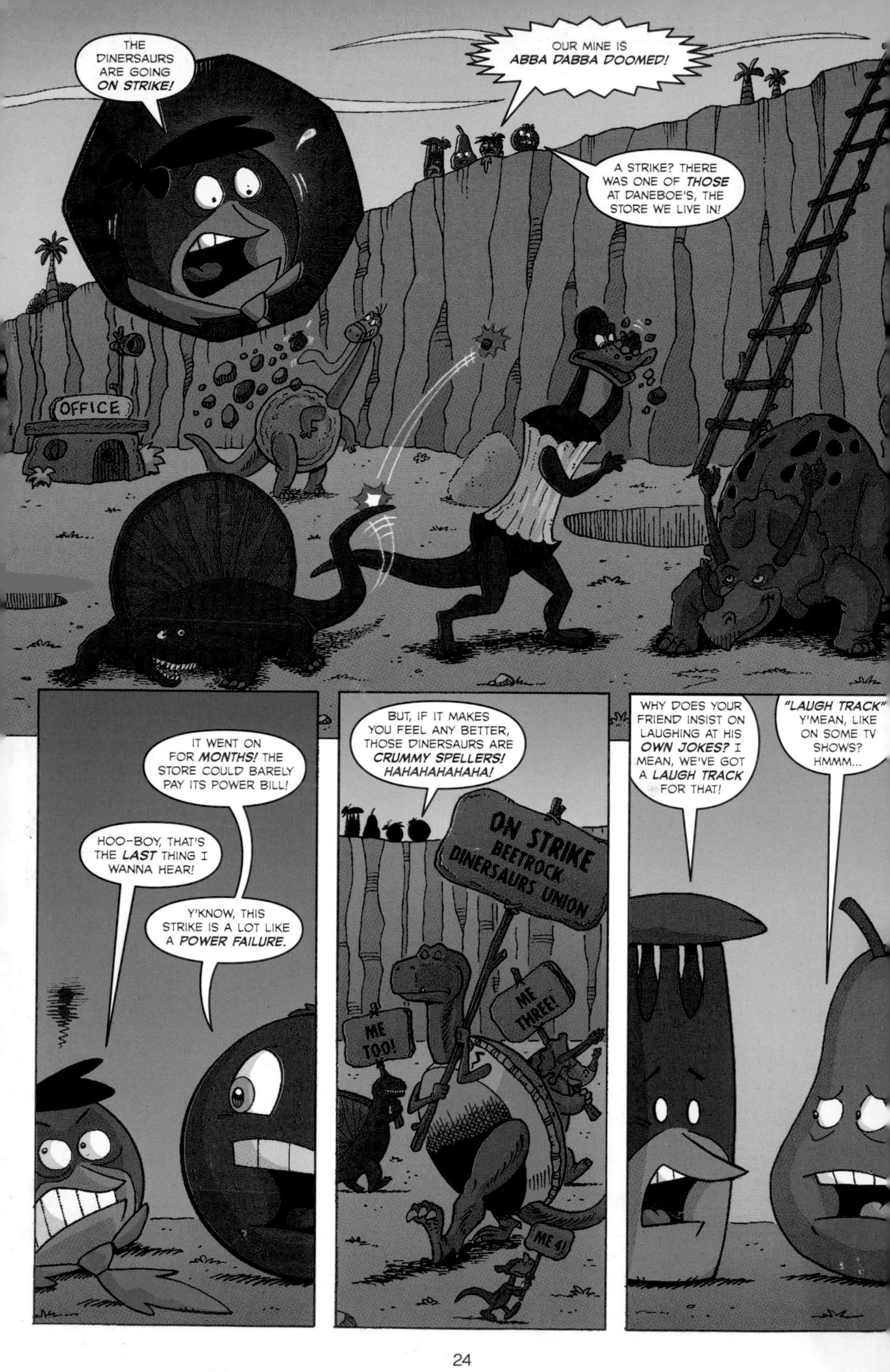
THE DINERSAURS ARE GOING ON STRIKE!
OUR MINE IS ABBA DABBA DOOMED!
A STRIKE? THERE WAS ONE OF THOSE AT DANEBOE'S, THE STORE WE LIVE IN!
OFFICE
IT WENT ON FOR MONTHS! THE STORE COULD BARELY PAY ITS POWER BILL!
HOO-BOY, THAT'S THE LAST THING I WANNA HEAR!
Y'KNOW, THIS STRIKE IS A LOT LIKE A POWER FAILURE.
BUT, IF IT MAKES YOU FEEL ANY BETTER, THOSE DINERSAURS ARE CRUMMY SPELLERS! HAHAHAHAHAHA!
ON STRIKE BEETROCK DINERSAURS UNION
ME TOO!
ME THREE!
ME 4!
WHY DOES YOUR FRIEND INSIST ON LAUGHING AT HIS OWN JOKES? I MEAN, WE'VE GOT A LAUGH TRACK FOR THAT!
"LAUGH TRACK" Y'MEAN, LIKE ON SOME TV SHOWS? HMMM...

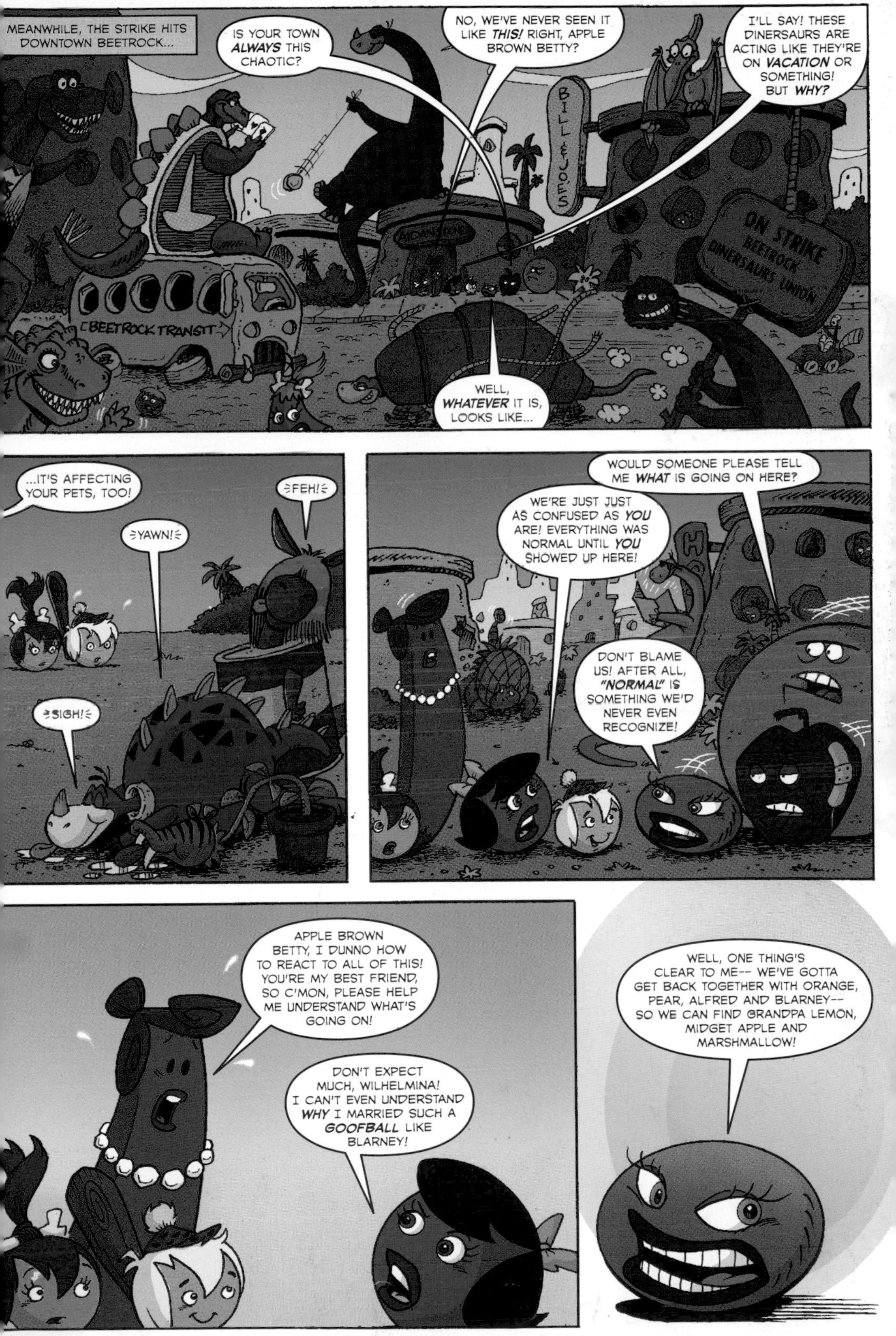

MEANWHILE, THE STRIKE HITS DOWNTOWN BEETROCK...
IS YOUR TOWN ALWAYS THIS CHAOTIC?
NO, WE'VE NEVER SEEN IT LIKE THIS! RIGHT, APPLE BROWN BETTY?
I'LL SAY! THESE DINERSAURS ARE ACTING LIKE THEY'RE ON VACATION OR SOMETHING! BUT WHY?
BILL & JOE'S
ON STRIKE BEETROCK DINERSAURS UNION
BEETROCK TRANSIT
WELL, WHATEVER IT IS, LOOKS LIKE...
...IT'S AFFECTING YOUR PETS, TOO!
FEH!
YAWN!
SIGH!
WOULD SOMEONE PLEASE TELL ME WHAT IS GOING ON HERE?
WE'RE JUST JUST AS CONFUSED AS YOU ARE! EVERYTHING WAS NORMAL UNTIL YOU SHOWED UP HERE!
DON'T BLAME US! AFTER ALL, "NORMAL" IS SOMETHING WE'D NEVER EVEN RECOGNIZE!
APPLE BROWN BETTY, I DUNNO HOW TO REACT TO ALL OF THIS! YOU'RE MY BEST FRIEND, SO C'MON, PLEASE HELP ME UNDERSTAND WHAT'S GOING ON!
DON'T EXPECT MUCH, WILHELMINA! I CAN'T EVEN UNDERSTAND WHY I MARRIED SUCH A GOOFBALL LIKE BLARNEY!
WELL, ONE THING'S CLEAR TO ME-- WE'VE GOTTA GET BACK TOGETHER WITH ORANGE, PEAR, ALFRED AND BLARNEY-- SO WE CAN FIND GRANDPA LEMON, MIDGET APPLE AND MARSHMALLOW!

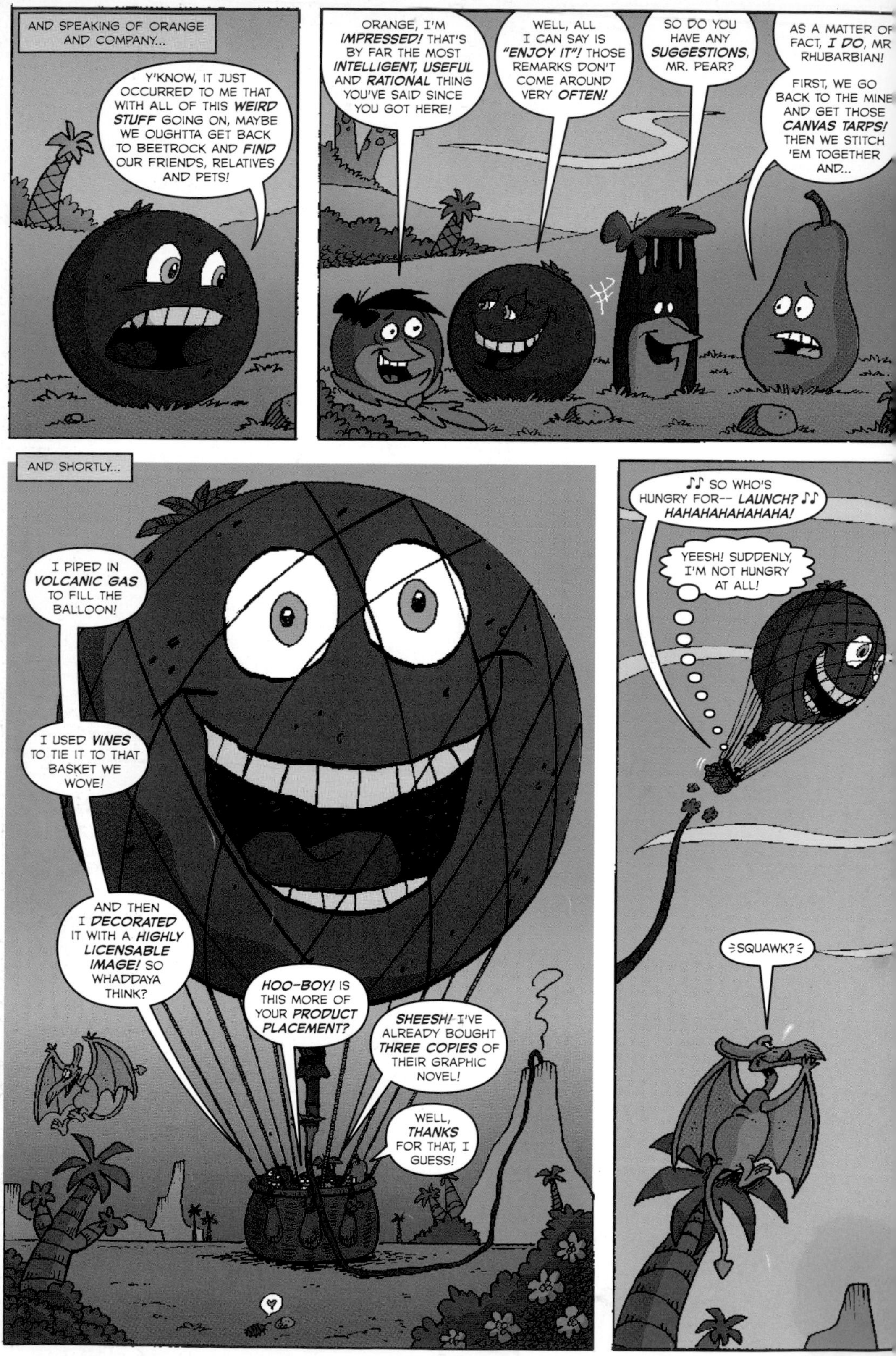

AND SPEAKING OF ORANGE AND COMPANY...
Y'KNOW, IT JUST OCCURRED TO ME THAT WITH ALL OF THIS WEIRD STUFF GOING ON, MAYBE WE OUGHTTA GET BACK TO BEETROCK AND FIND OUR FRIENDS, RELATIVES AND PETS!
ORANGE, I'M IMPRESSED! THAT'S BY FAR THE MOST INTELLIGENT, USEFUL AND RATIONAL THING YOU'VE SAID SINCE YOU GOT HERE!
WELL, ALL I CAN SAY IS "ENJOY IT"! THOSE REMARKS DON'T COME AROUND VERY OFTEN!
SO DO YOU HAVE ANY SUGGESTIONS, MR. PEAR?
AS A MATTER OF FACT, I DO, MR RHUBARBIAN!
FIRST, WE GO BACK TO THE MINE AND GET THOSE CANVAS TARPS! THEN WE STITCH 'EM TOGETHER AND...
AND SHORTLY...
I PIPED IN VOLCANIC GAS TO FILL THE BALLOON!
I USED VINES TO TIE IT TO THAT BASKET WE WOVE!
AND THEN I DECORATED IT WITH A HIGHLY LICENSABLE IMAGE! SO WHADDAYA THINK?
HOO-BOY! IS THIS MORE OF YOUR PRODUCT PLACEMENT?
SHEESH! I'VE ALREADY BOUGHT THREE COPIES OF THEIR GRAPHIC NOVEL!
WELL, THANKS FOR THAT, I GUESS!
♪♪ SO WHO'S HUNGRY FOR-- LAUNCH? ♪♪ HAHAHAHAHAHAHAHA!
YEESH! SUDDENLY, I'M NOT HUNGRY AT ALL!
SQUAWK?

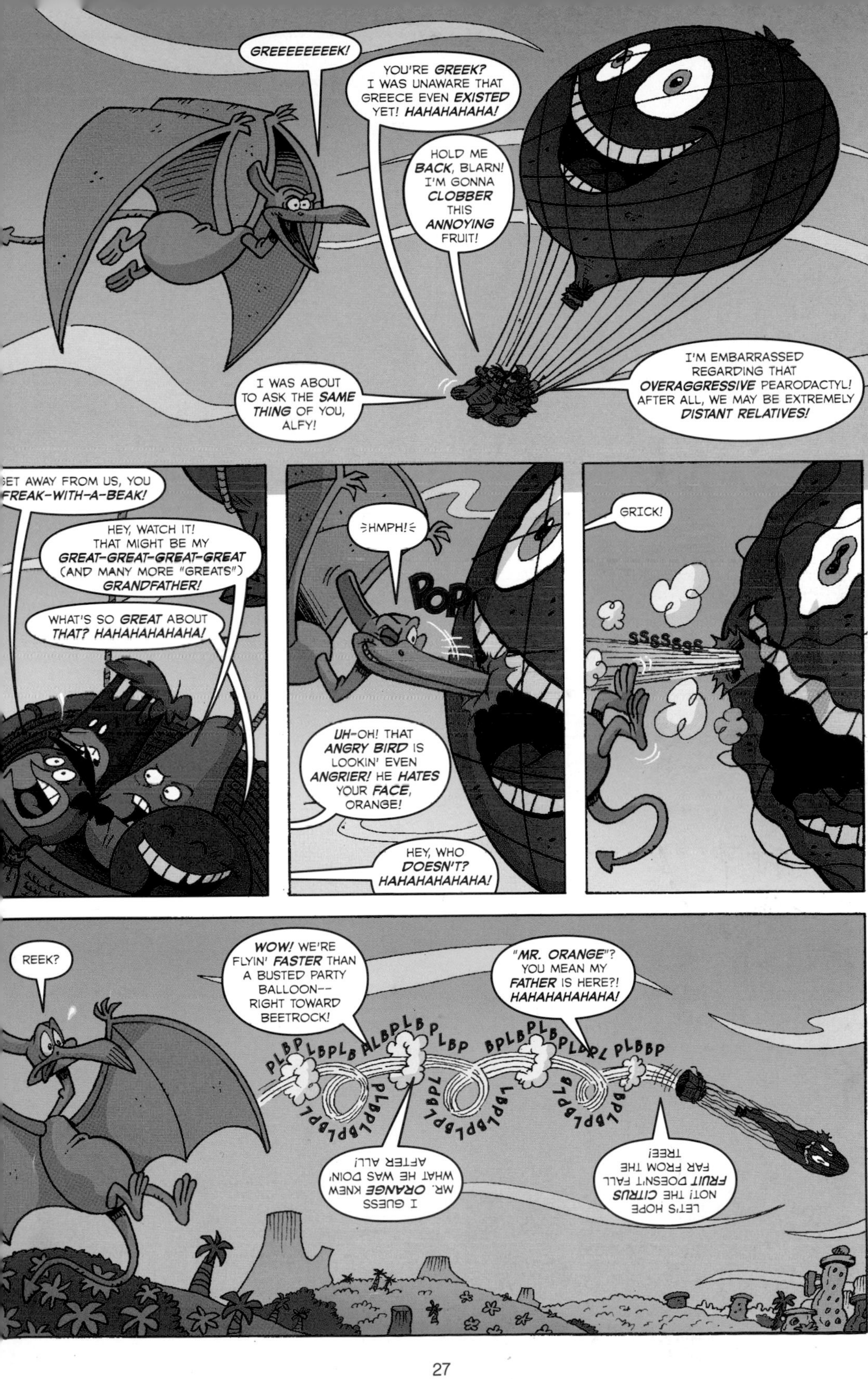
GREEEEEEEEK!
YOU'RE GREEK? I WAS UNAWARE THAT GREECE EVEN EXISTED YET! HAHAHAHAHA!
HOLD ME BACK, BLARN! I'M GONNA CLOBBER THIS ANNOYING FRUIT!
I WAS ABOUT TO ASK THE SAME THING OF YOU, ALFY!
I'M EMBARRASSED REGARDING THAT OVERAGGRESSIVE PEARODACTYL! AFTER ALL, WE MAY BE EXTREMELY DISTANT RELATIVES!
GET AWAY FROM US, YOU FREAK-WITH-A-BEAK!
HEY, WATCH IT! THAT MIGHT BE MY GREAT-GREAT-GREAT-GREAT (AND MANY MORE "GREATS") GRANDFATHER!
WHAT'S SO GREAT ABOUT THAT? HAHAHAHAHAHA!
HMPH!
POP!
UH-OH! THAT ANGRY BIRD IS LOOKIN' EVEN ANGRIER! HE HATES YOUR FACE, ORANGE!
HEY, WHO DOESN'T? HAHAHAHAHAHA!
GRICK!
SSSSSSS
REEK?
WOW! WE'RE FLYIN' FASTER THAN A BUSTED PARTY BALLOON-- RIGHT TOWARD BEETROCK!
"MR. ORANGE"? YOU MEAN MY FATHER IS HERE?! HAHAHAHAHAHA!
I GUESS MR. ORANGE KNEW WHAT HE WAS DOIN' AFTER ALL!
LET'S HOPE NOT! THE CITRUS FRUIT DOESN'T FALL FAR FROM THE TREE!

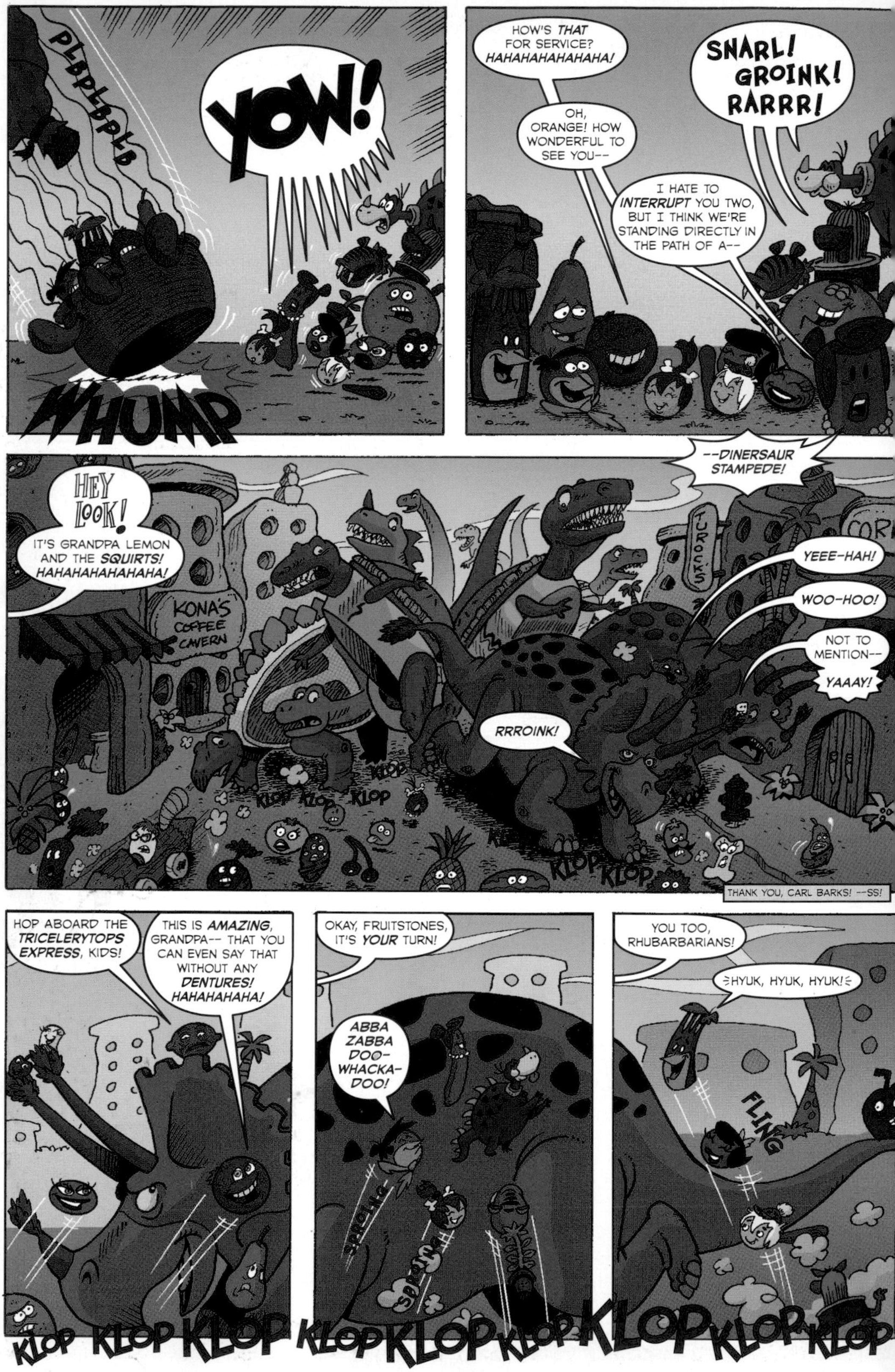
PLBPLBPLB
YOW!
WHUMP
HOW'S THAT FOR SERVICE? HAHAHAHAHAHAHA!
OH, ORANGE! HOW WONDERFUL TO SEE YOU--
SNARL! GROINK! RARRR!
I HATE TO INTERRUPT YOU TWO, BUT I THINK WE'RE STANDING DIRECTLY IN THE PATH OF A--
--DINERSAUR STAMPEDE!
HEY LOOK! IT'S GRANDPA LEMON AND THE SQUIRTS! HAHAHAHAHAHAHA!
KONA'S COFFEE CAVERN
TUROCKS
YEEE-HAH!
WOO-HOO!
NOT TO MENTION--
YAAAY!
RRROINK!
KLOP KLOP KLOP KLOP
KLOP KLOP
THANK YOU, CARL BARKS! --SS!
HOP ABOARD THE TRICELERYTOPS EXPRESS, KIDS!
THIS IS AMAZING, GRANDPA-- THAT YOU CAN EVEN SAY THAT WITHOUT ANY DENTURES! HAHAHAHAHA!
OKAY, FRUITSTONES, IT'S YOUR TURN!
ABBA ZABBA DOO-WHACKA-DOO!
SPROING
SPROING
YOU TOO, RHUBARBARIANS!
HYUK, HYUK, HYUK!
FLING
KLOP KLOP KLOP KLOP KLOP KLOP KLOP KLOP KLOP

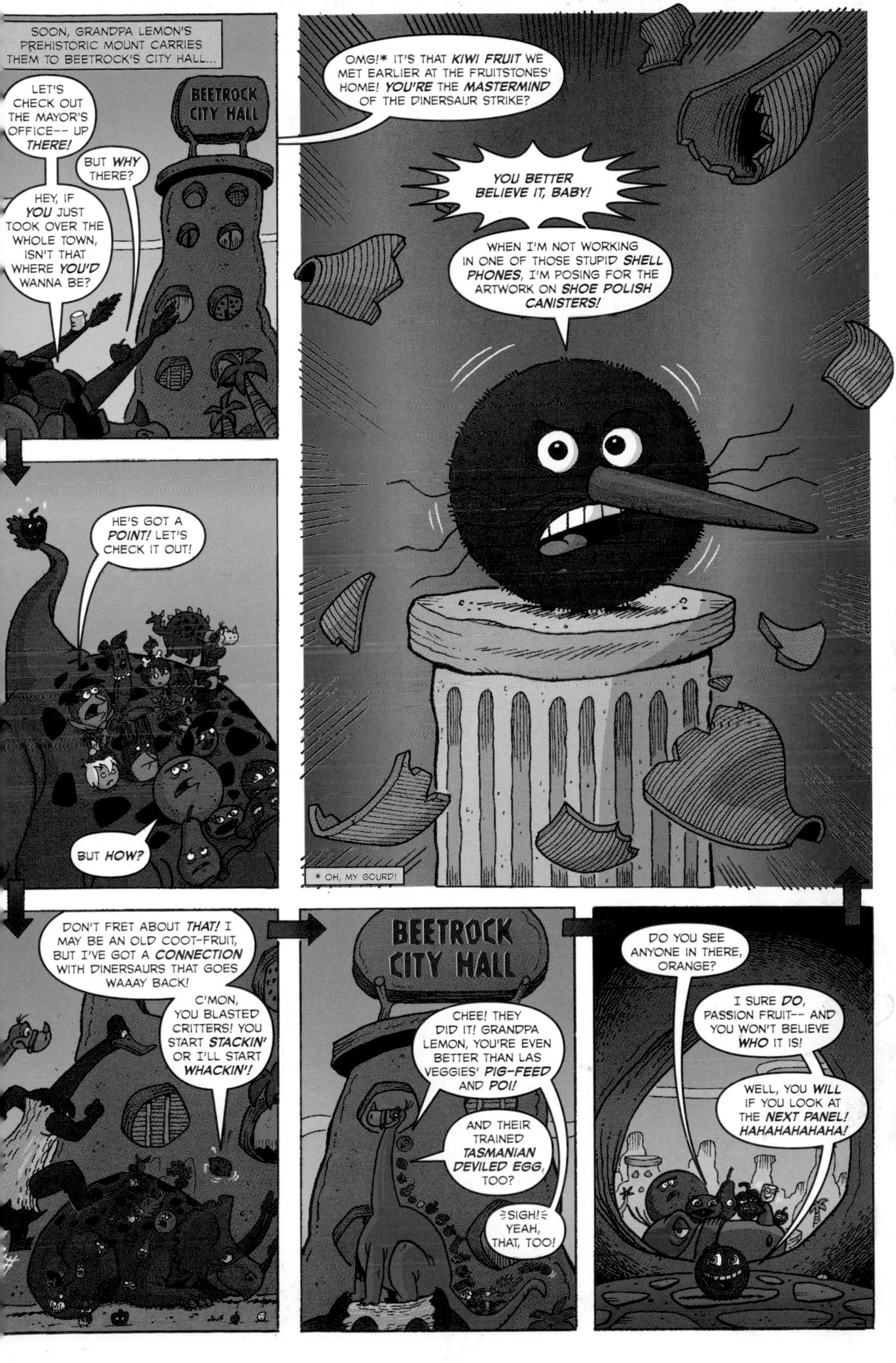

SOON, GRANDPA LEMON'S PREHISTORIC MOUNT CARRIES THEM TO BEETROCK'S CITY HALL...
BEETROCK CITY HALL
LET'S CHECK OUT THE MAYOR'S OFFICE-- UP THERE!
BUT WHY THERE?
HEY, IF YOU JUST TOOK OVER THE WHOLE TOWN, ISN'T THAT WHERE YOU'D WANNA BE?
OMG!* IT'S THAT KIWI FRUIT WE MET EARLIER AT THE FRUITSTONES' HOME! YOU'RE THE MASTERMIND OF THE DINERSAUR STRIKE?
YOU BETTER BELIEVE IT, BABY!
WHEN I'M NOT WORKING IN ONE OF THOSE STUPID SHELL PHONES, I'M POSING FOR THE ARTWORK ON SHOE POLISH CANISTERS!
* OH, MY GOURD!
HE'S GOT A POINT! LET'S CHECK IT OUT!
BUT HOW?
DON'T FRET ABOUT THAT! I MAY BE AN OLD COOT-FRUIT, BUT I'VE GOT A CONNECTION WITH DINERSAURS THAT GOES WAAAY BACK!
C'MON, YOU BLASTED CRITTERS! YOU START STACKIN' OR I'LL START WHACKIN'!
BEETROCK CITY HALL
CHEE! THEY DID IT! GRANDPA LEMON, YOU'RE EVEN BETTER THAN LAS VEGGIES' PIG-FEED AND POI!
AND THEIR TRAINED TASMANIAN DEVILED EGG, TOO?
SIGH! YEAH, THAT, TOO!
DO YOU SEE ANYONE IN THERE, ORANGE?
I SURE DO, PASSION FRUIT-- AND YOU WON'T BELIEVE WHO IT IS!
WELL, YOU WILL IF YOU LOOK AT THE NEXT PANEL! HAHAHAHAHAHA!

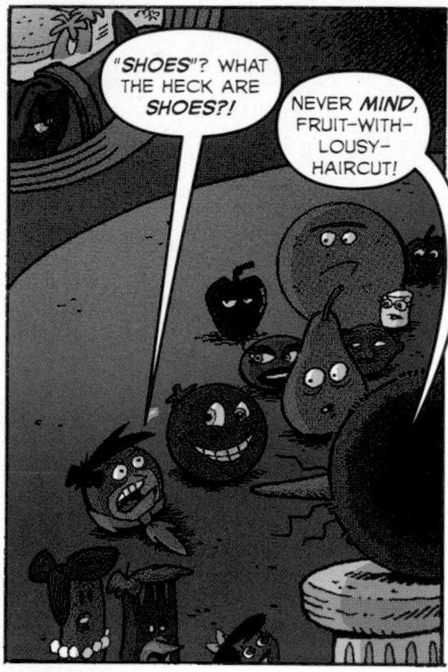
"*SHOES*"? WHAT THE HECK ARE *SHOES?!*
NEVER *MIND*, FRUIT-WITH-LOUSY-HAIRCUT!

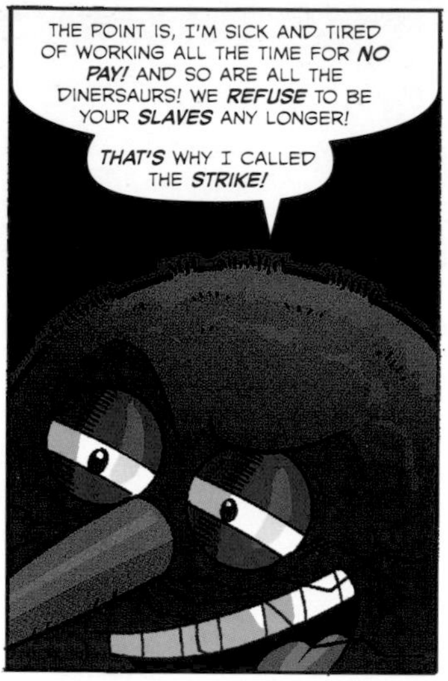
THE POINT IS, I'M SICK AND TIRED OF WORKING ALL THE TIME FOR *NO PAY!* AND SO ARE ALL THE DINERSAURS! WE *REFUSE* TO BE YOUR *SLAVES* ANY LONGER!
THAT'S WHY I CALLED THE *STRIKE!*

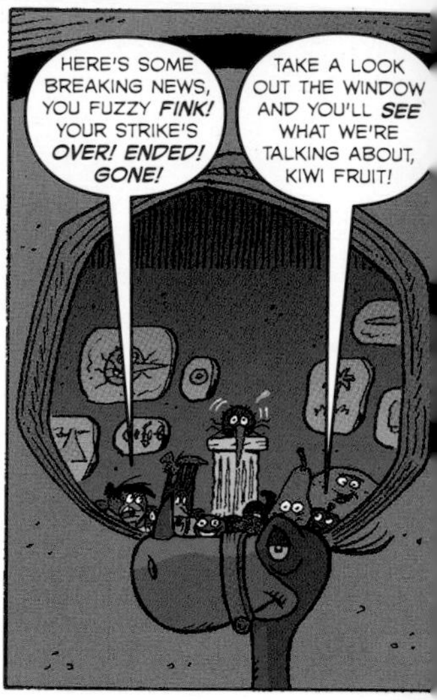
HERE'S SOME BREAKING NEWS, YOU FUZZY *FINK!* YOUR STRIKE'S *OVER! ENDED! GONE!*
TAKE A LOOK OUT THE WINDOW AND YOU'LL *SEE* WHAT WE'RE TALKING ABOUT, KIWI FRUIT!

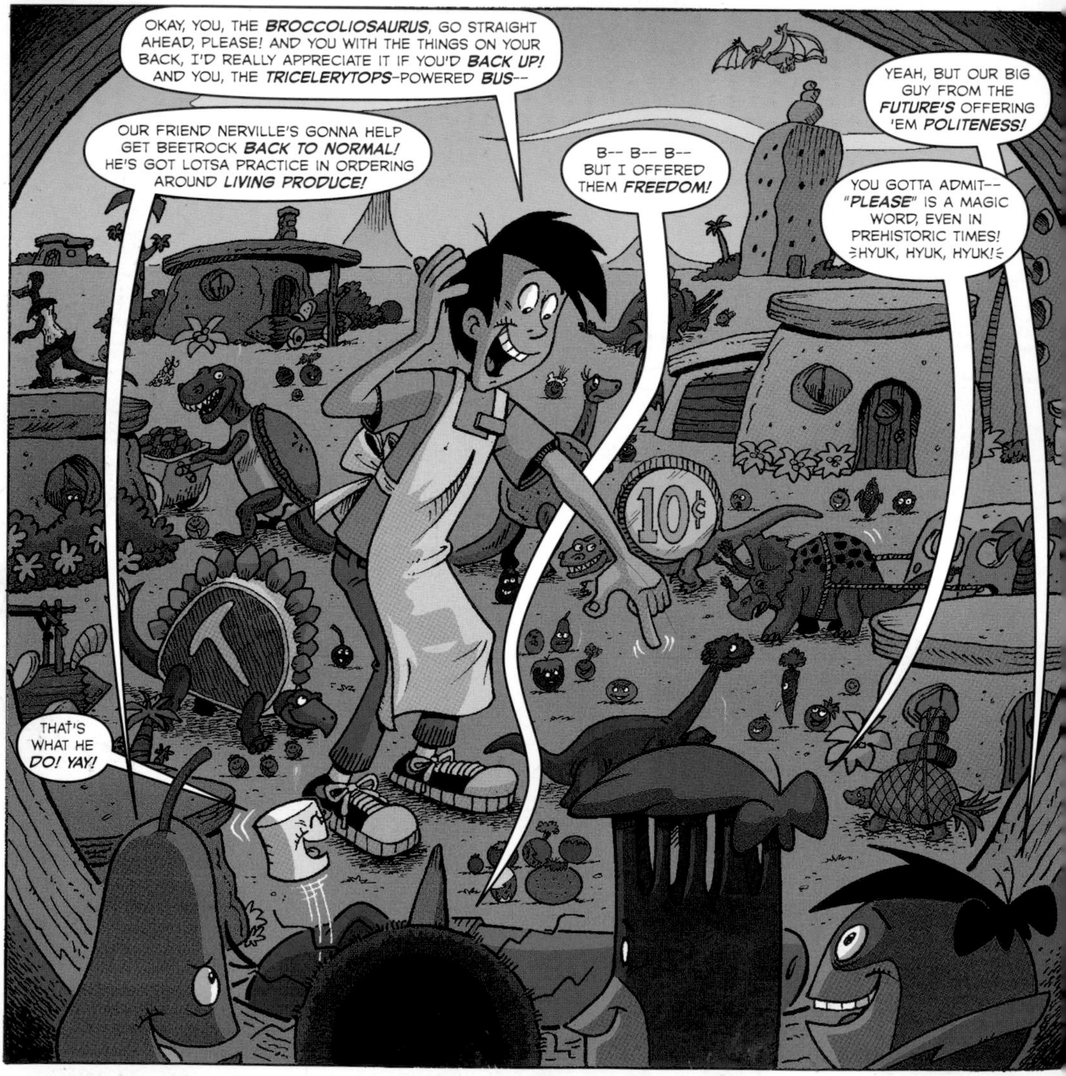
OKAY, YOU, THE *BROCCOLIOSAURUS*, GO STRAIGHT AHEAD, PLEASE! AND YOU WITH THE THINGS ON YOUR BACK, I'D REALLY APPRECIATE IT IF YOU'D *BACK UP!* AND YOU, THE *TRICELERYTOPS*-POWERED *BUS*--
OUR FRIEND NERVILLE'S GONNA HELP GET BEETROCK *BACK TO NORMAL!* HE'S GOT LOTSA PRACTICE IN ORDERING AROUND *LIVING PRODUCE!*
B-- B-- B-- BUT I OFFERED THEM *FREEDOM!*
YEAH, BUT OUR BIG GUY FROM THE *FUTURE'S* OFFERING 'EM *POLITENESS!*
YOU GOTTA ADMIT-- "*PLEASE*" IS A MAGIC WORD, EVEN IN PREHISTORIC TIMES! HYUK, HYUK, HYUK!
10¢
THAT'S WHAT HE *DO! YAY!*

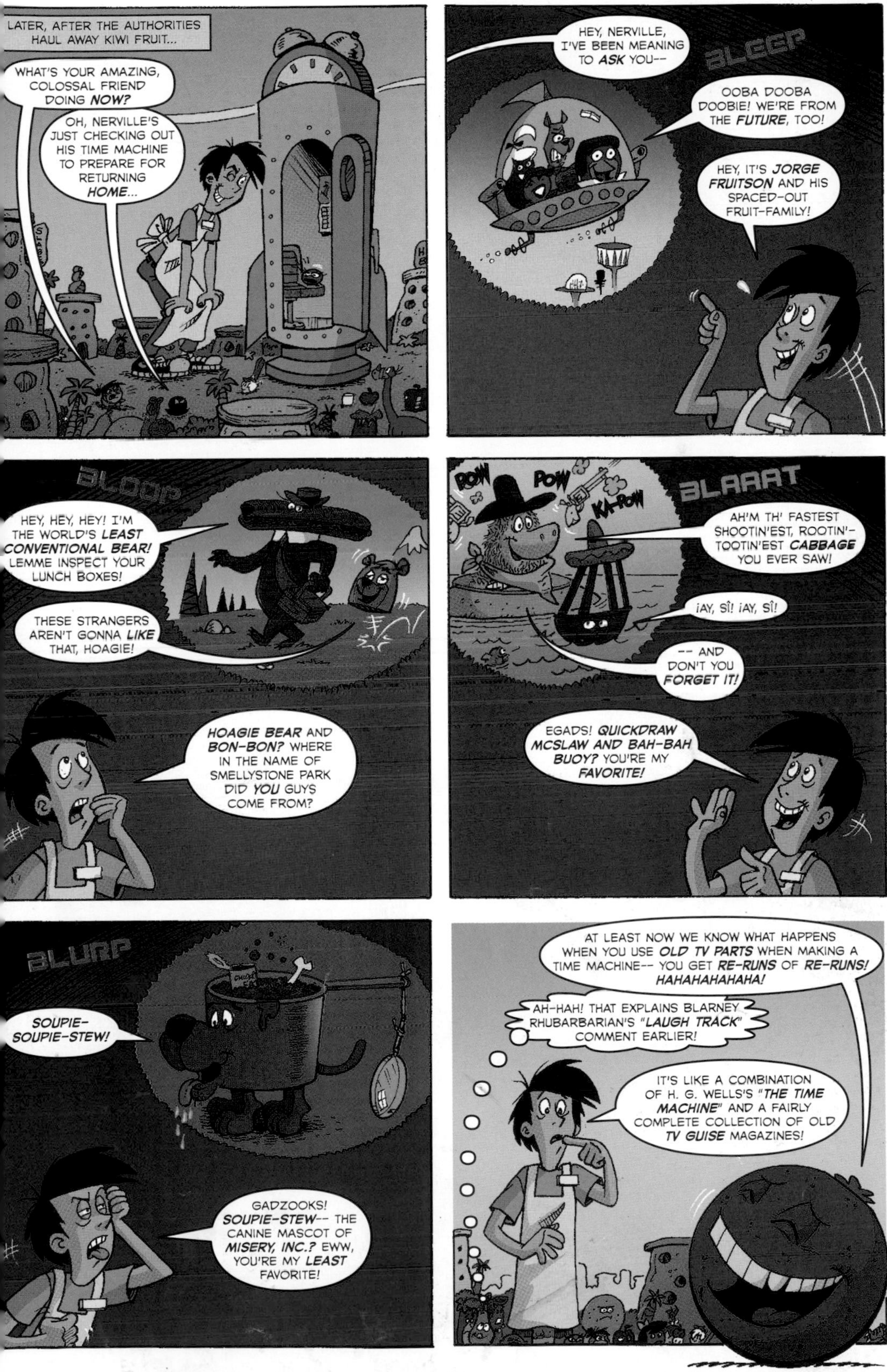
LATER, AFTER THE AUTHORITIES HAUL AWAY KIWI FRUIT...
WHAT'S YOUR AMAZING, COLOSSAL FRIEND DOING NOW?
OH, NERVILLE'S JUST CHECKING OUT HIS TIME MACHINE TO PREPARE FOR RETURNING HOME...
HEY, NERVILLE, I'VE BEEN MEANING TO ASK YOU--
BLEEP
OOBA DOOBA DOOBIE! WE'RE FROM THE FUTURE, TOO!
HEY, IT'S JORGE FRUITSON AND HIS SPACED-OUT FRUIT-FAMILY!
BLOOP
HEY, HEY, HEY! I'M THE WORLD'S LEAST CONVENTIONAL BEAR! LEMME INSPECT YOUR LUNCH BOXES!
THESE STRANGERS AREN'T GONNA LIKE THAT, HOAGIE!
HOAGIE BEAR AND BON-BON? WHERE IN THE NAME OF SMELLYSTONE PARK DID YOU GUYS COME FROM?
POW
POW
KA-POW
BLAAAT
AH'M TH' FASTEST SHOOTIN'EST, ROOTIN'-TOOTIN'EST CABBAGE YOU EVER SAW!
¡AY, SÍ! ¡AY, SÍ!
-- AND DON'T YOU FORGET IT!
EGADS! QUICKDRAW MCSLAW AND BAH-BAH BUOY? YOU'RE MY FAVORITE!
BLURP
SOUPIE-SOUPIE-STEW!
GADZOOKS! SOUPIE-STEW-- THE CANINE MASCOT OF MISERY, INC.? EWW, YOU'RE MY LEAST FAVORITE!
AT LEAST NOW WE KNOW WHAT HAPPENS WHEN YOU USE OLD TV PARTS WHEN MAKING A TIME MACHINE-- YOU GET RE-RUNS OF RE-RUNS! HAHAHAHAHAHA!
AH-HAH! THAT EXPLAINS BLARNEY RHUBARBARIAN'S "LAUGH TRACK" COMMENT EARLIER!
IT'S LIKE A COMBINATION OF H. G. WELLS'S "THE TIME MACHINE" AND A FAIRLY COMPLETE COLLECTION OF OLD TV GUISE MAGAZINES!

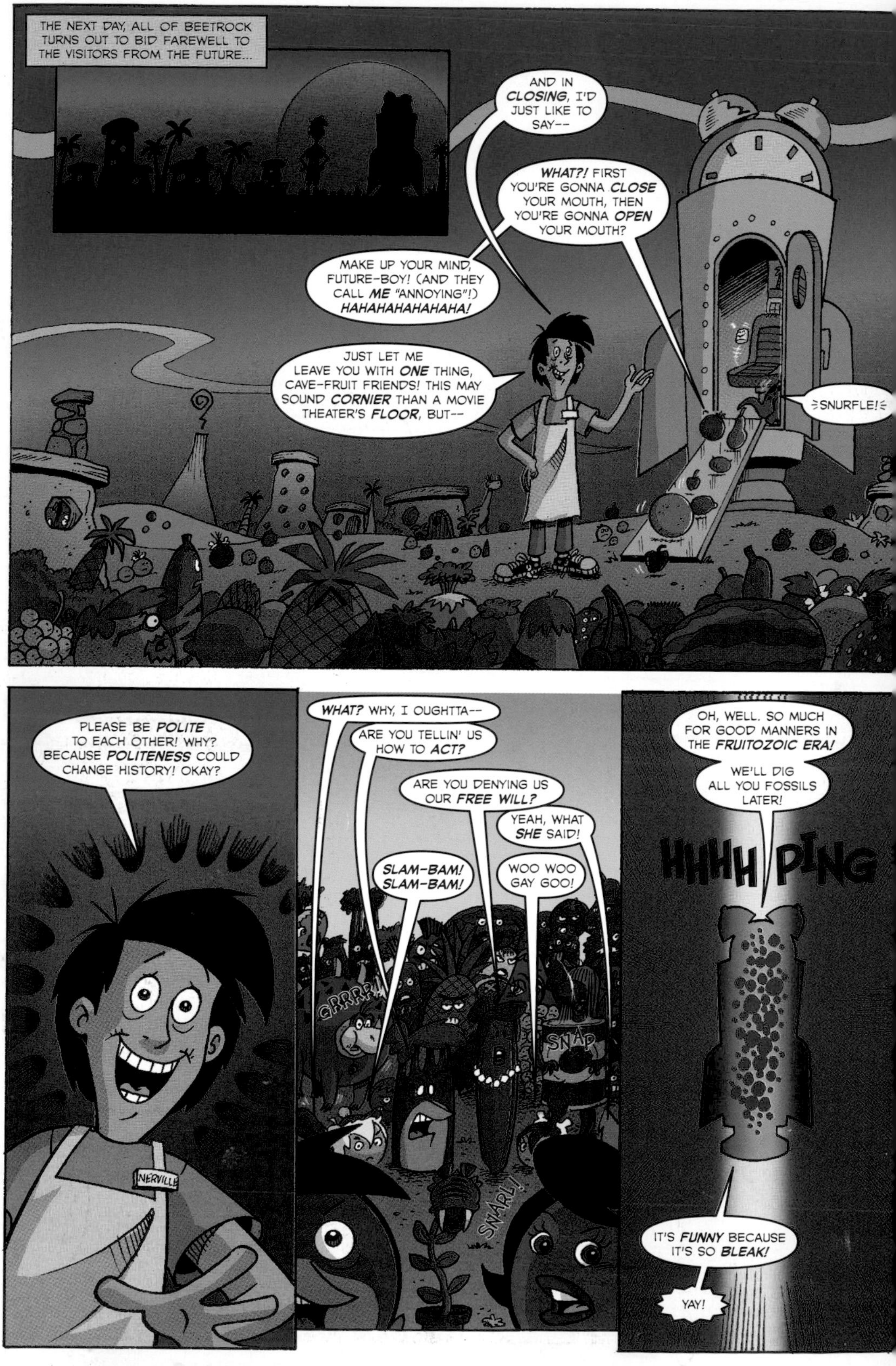
THE NEXT DAY, ALL OF BEETROCK TURNS OUT TO BID FAREWELL TO THE VISITORS FROM THE FUTURE...
AND IN CLOSING, I'D JUST LIKE TO SAY--
WHAT?! FIRST YOU'RE GONNA CLOSE YOUR MOUTH, THEN YOU'RE GONNA OPEN YOUR MOUTH?
MAKE UP YOUR MIND, FUTURE-BOY! (AND THEY CALL ME "ANNOYING"!) HAHAHAHAHAHAHA!
JUST LET ME LEAVE YOU WITH ONE THING, CAVE-FRUIT FRIENDS! THIS MAY SOUND CORNIER THAN A MOVIE THEATER'S FLOOR, BUT--
SNURFLE!
PLEASE BE POLITE TO EACH OTHER! WHY? BECAUSE POLITENESS COULD CHANGE HISTORY! OKAY?
NERVILLE
WHAT? WHY, I OUGHTTA--
ARE YOU TELLIN' US HOW TO ACT?
ARE YOU DENYING US OUR FREE WILL?
YEAH, WHAT SHE SAID!
SLAM-BAM! SLAM-BAM!
WOO WOO GAY GOO!
SNAP
SNARL!
OH, WELL. SO MUCH FOR GOOD MANNERS IN THE FRUITOZOIC ERA!
WE'LL DIG ALL YOU FOSSILS LATER!
HHHH PING
IT'S FUNNY BECAUSE IT'S SO BLEAK!
YAY!

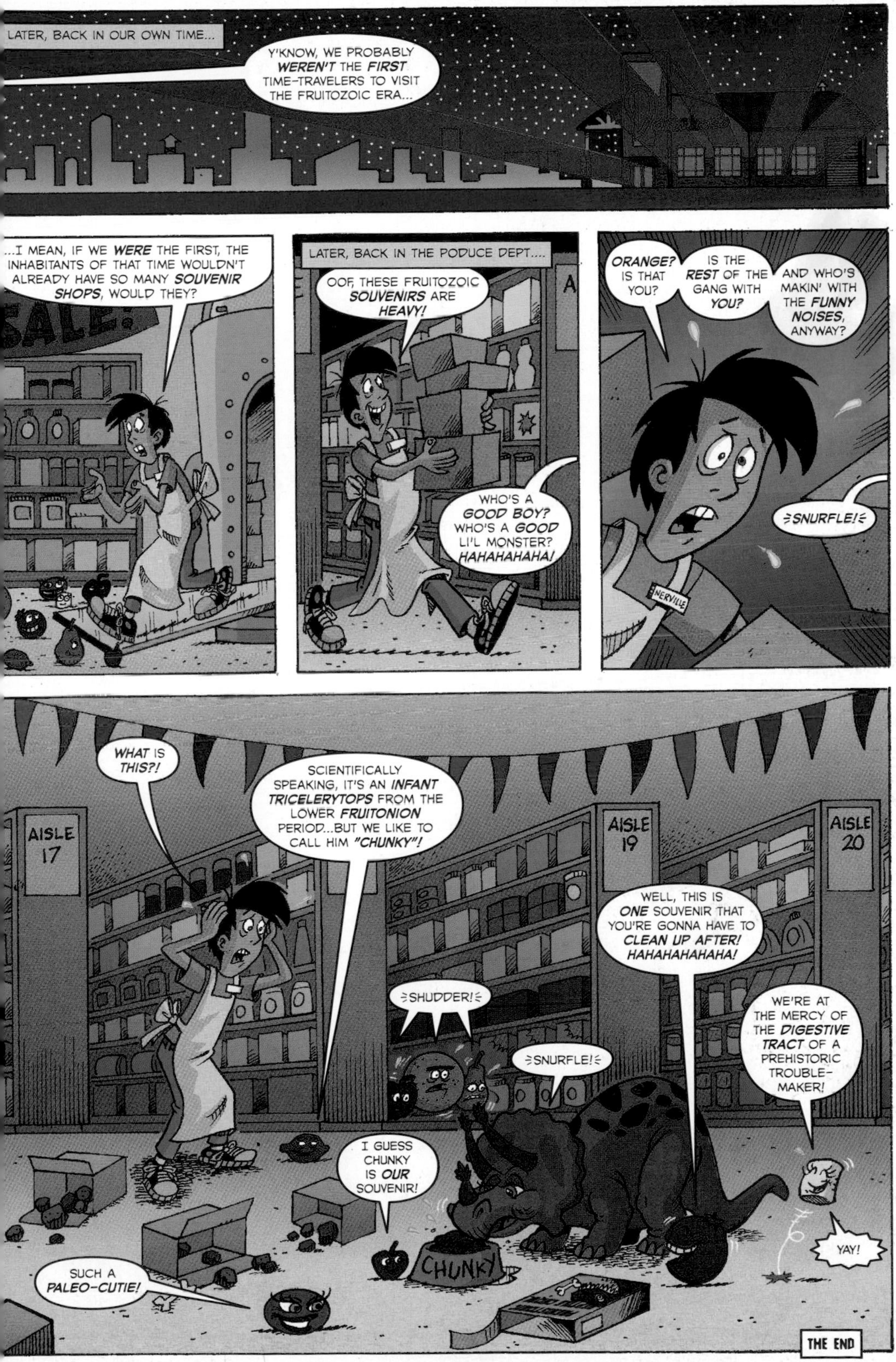
LATER, BACK IN OUR OWN TIME...
Y'KNOW, WE PROBABLY WEREN'T THE FIRST TIME-TRAVELERS TO VISIT THE FRUITOZOIC ERA...
...I MEAN, IF WE WERE THE FIRST, THE INHABITANTS OF THAT TIME WOULDN'T ALREADY HAVE SO MANY SOUVENIR SHOPS, WOULD THEY?
LATER, BACK IN THE PODUCE DEPT....
OOF, THESE FRUITOZOIC SOUVENIRS ARE HEAVY!
WHO'S A GOOD BOY? WHO'S A GOOD LI'L MONSTER? HAHAHAHAHA!
ORANGE? IS THAT YOU?
IS THE REST OF THE GANG WITH YOU?
AND WHO'S MAKIN' WITH THE FUNNY NOISES, ANYWAY?
SNURFLE!
NERVILLE
WHAT IS THIS?!
SCIENTIFICALLY SPEAKING, IT'S AN INFANT TRICELERYTOPS FROM THE LOWER FRUITONION PERIOD...BUT WE LIKE TO CALL HIM "CHUNKY"!
AISLE 17
AISLE 19
AISLE 20
WELL, THIS IS ONE SOUVENIR THAT YOU'RE GONNA HAVE TO CLEAN UP AFTER! HAHAHAHAHAHA!
SHUDDER!
WE'RE AT THE MERCY OF THE DIGESTIVE TRACT OF A PREHISTORIC TROUBLE-MAKER!
SNURFLE!
I GUESS CHUNKY IS OUR SOUVENIR!
CHUNKY
YAY!
SUCH A PALEO-CUTIE!
THE END

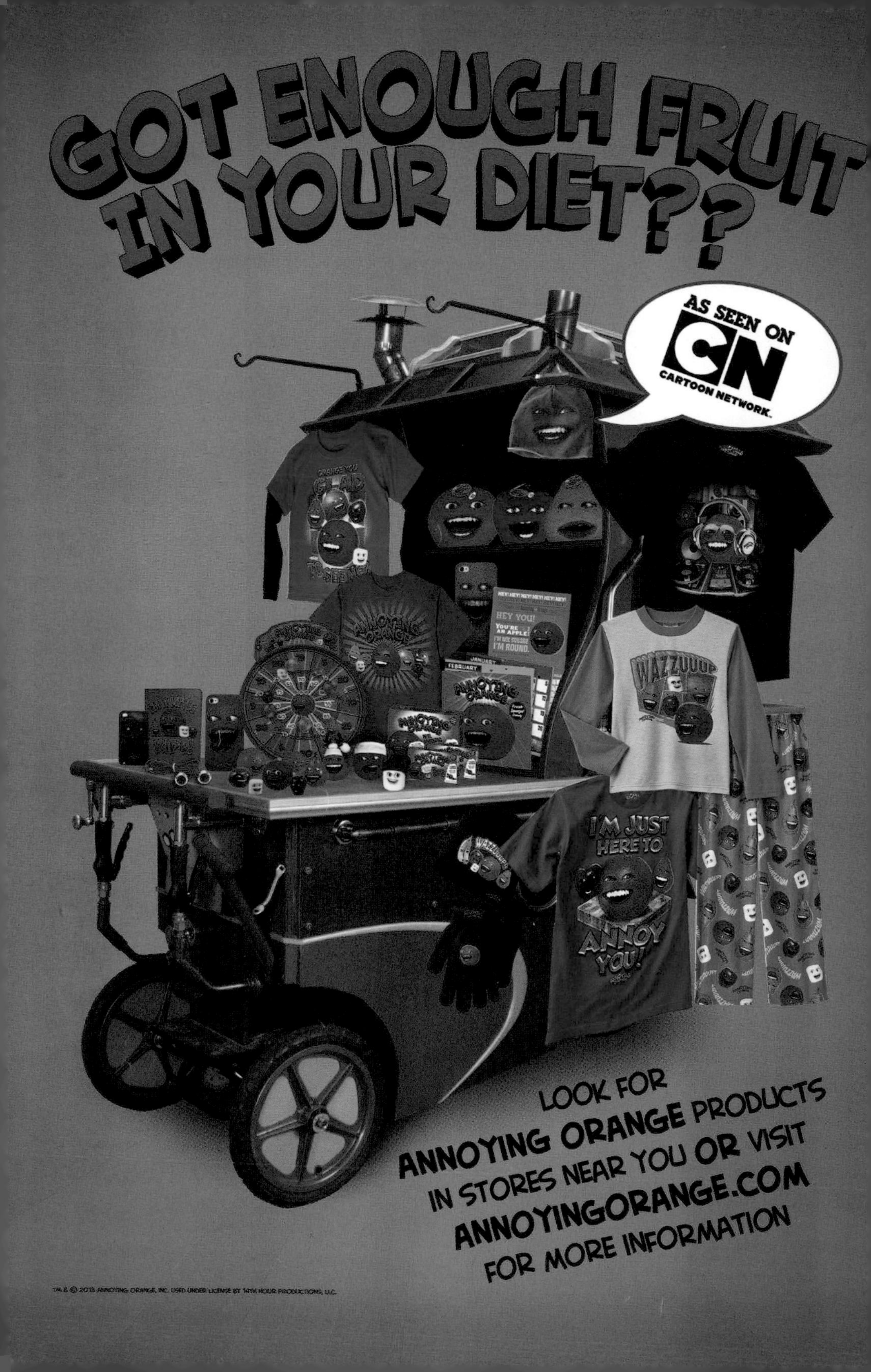

GOT ENOUGH FRUIT IN YOUR DIET??
AS SEEN ON
CN
CARTOON NETWORK.
LOOK FOR
ANNOYING ORANGE PRODUCTS
IN STORES NEAR YOU OR VISIT
ANNOYINGORANGE.COM
FOR MORE INFORMATION

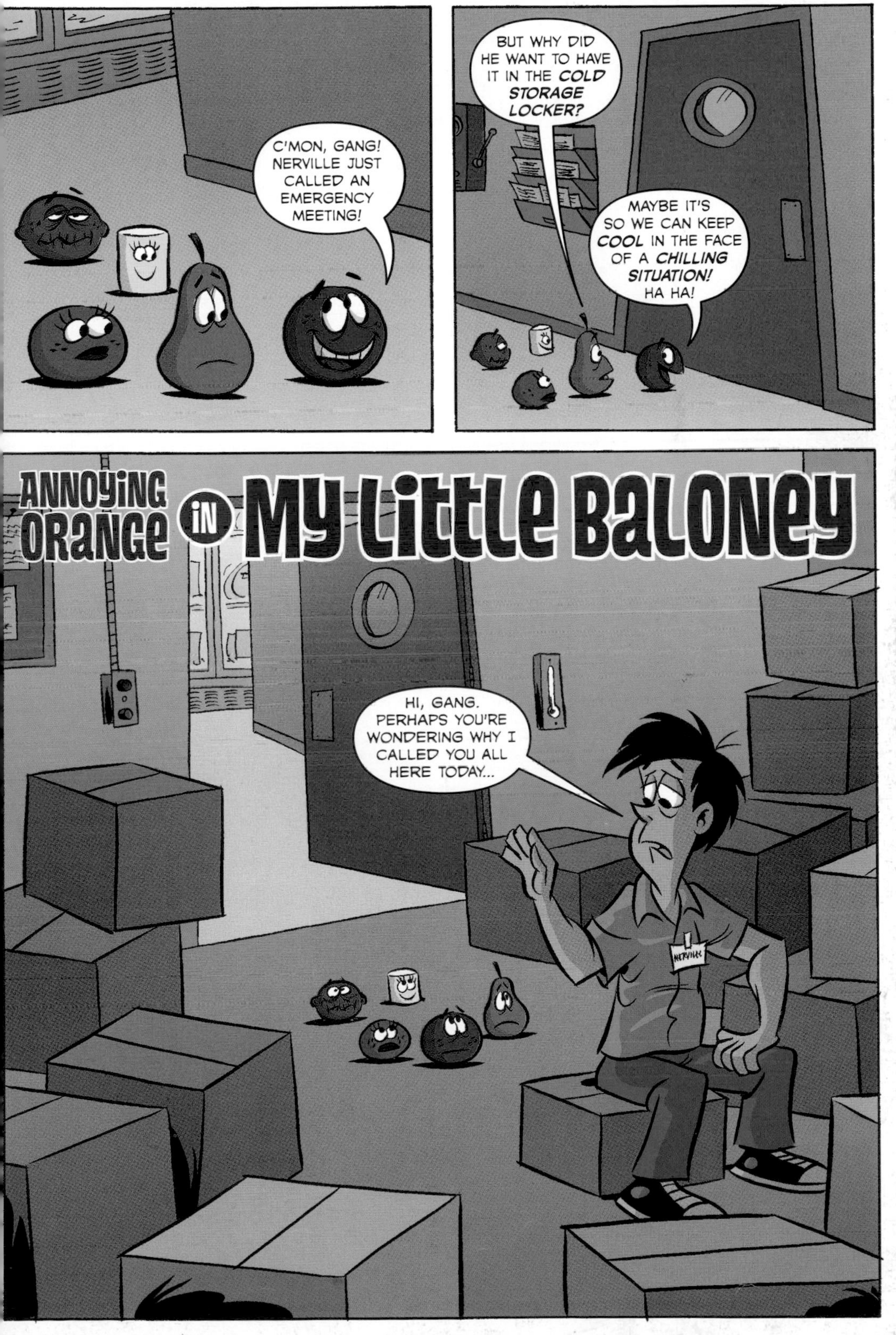
C'MON, GANG! NERVILLE JUST CALLED AN EMERGENCY MEETING!
BUT WHY DID HE WANT TO HAVE IT IN THE COLD STORAGE LOCKER?
MAYBE IT'S SO WE CAN KEEP COOL IN THE FACE OF A CHILLING SITUATION! HA HA!
ANNOYING ORANGE IN MY LITTLE BALONEY
HI, GANG. PERHAPS YOU'RE WONDERING WHY I CALLED YOU ALL HERE TODAY...

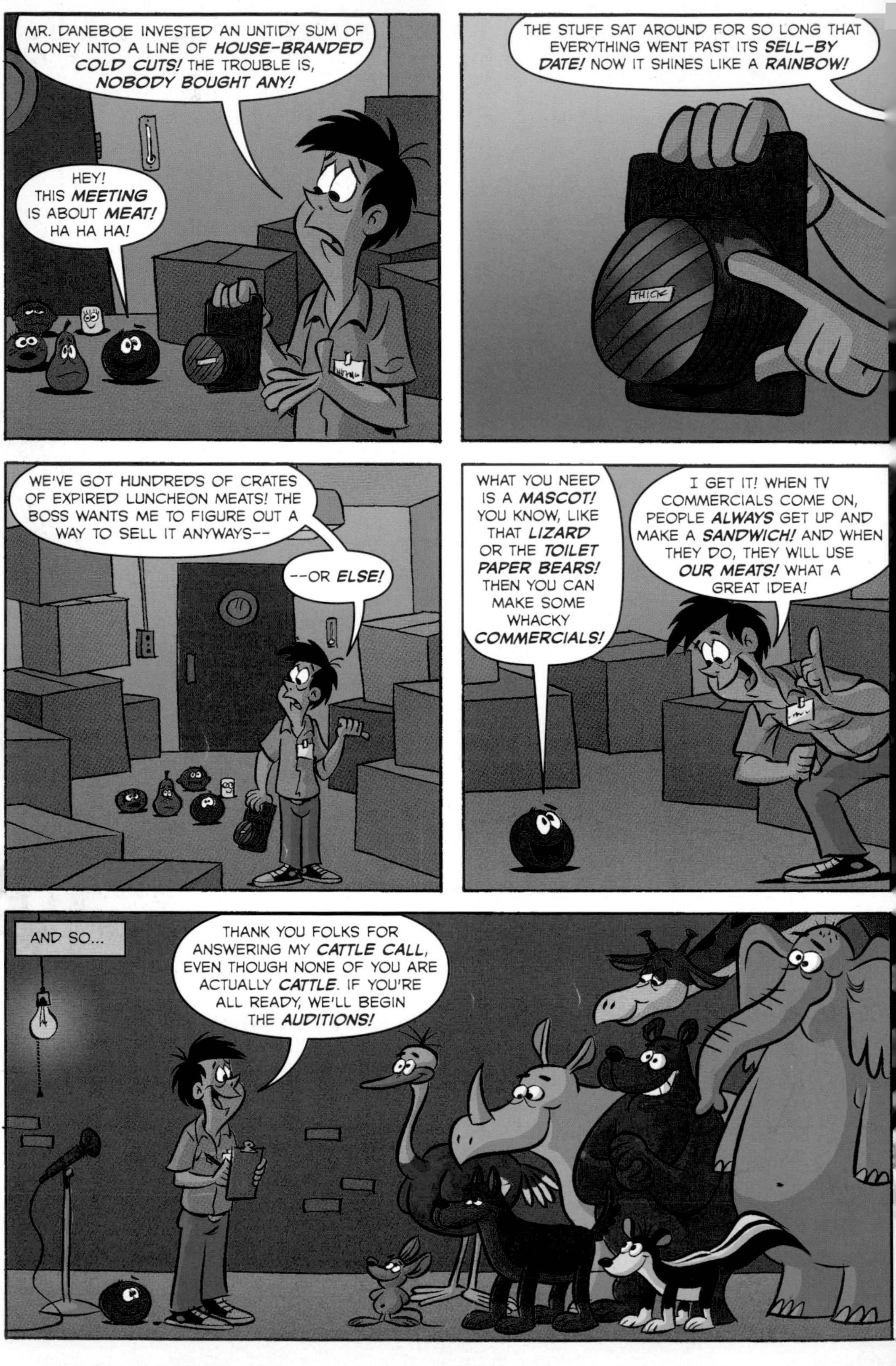
MR. DANEBOE INVESTED AN UNTIDY SUM OF MONEY INTO A LINE OF HOUSE-BRANDED COLD CUTS! THE TROUBLE IS, NOBODY BOUGHT ANY!
HEY! THIS MEETING IS ABOUT MEAT! HA HA HA!
THE STUFF SAT AROUND FOR SO LONG THAT EVERYTHING WENT PAST ITS SELL-BY DATE! NOW IT SHINES LIKE A RAINBOW!
THICK
WE'VE GOT HUNDREDS OF CRATES OF EXPIRED LUNCHEON MEATS! THE BOSS WANTS ME TO FIGURE OUT A WAY TO SELL IT ANYWAYS--
--OR ELSE!
WHAT YOU NEED IS A MASCOT! YOU KNOW, LIKE THAT LIZARD OR THE TOILET PAPER BEARS! THEN YOU CAN MAKE SOME WHACKY COMMERCIALS!
I GET IT! WHEN TV COMMERCIALS COME ON, PEOPLE ALWAYS GET UP AND MAKE A SANDWICH! AND WHEN THEY DO, THEY WILL USE OUR MEATS! WHAT A GREAT IDEA!
AND SO...
THANK YOU FOLKS FOR ANSWERING MY CATTLE CALL, EVEN THOUGH NONE OF YOU ARE ACTUALLY CATTLE. IF YOU'RE ALL READY, WE'LL BEGIN THE AUDITIONS!

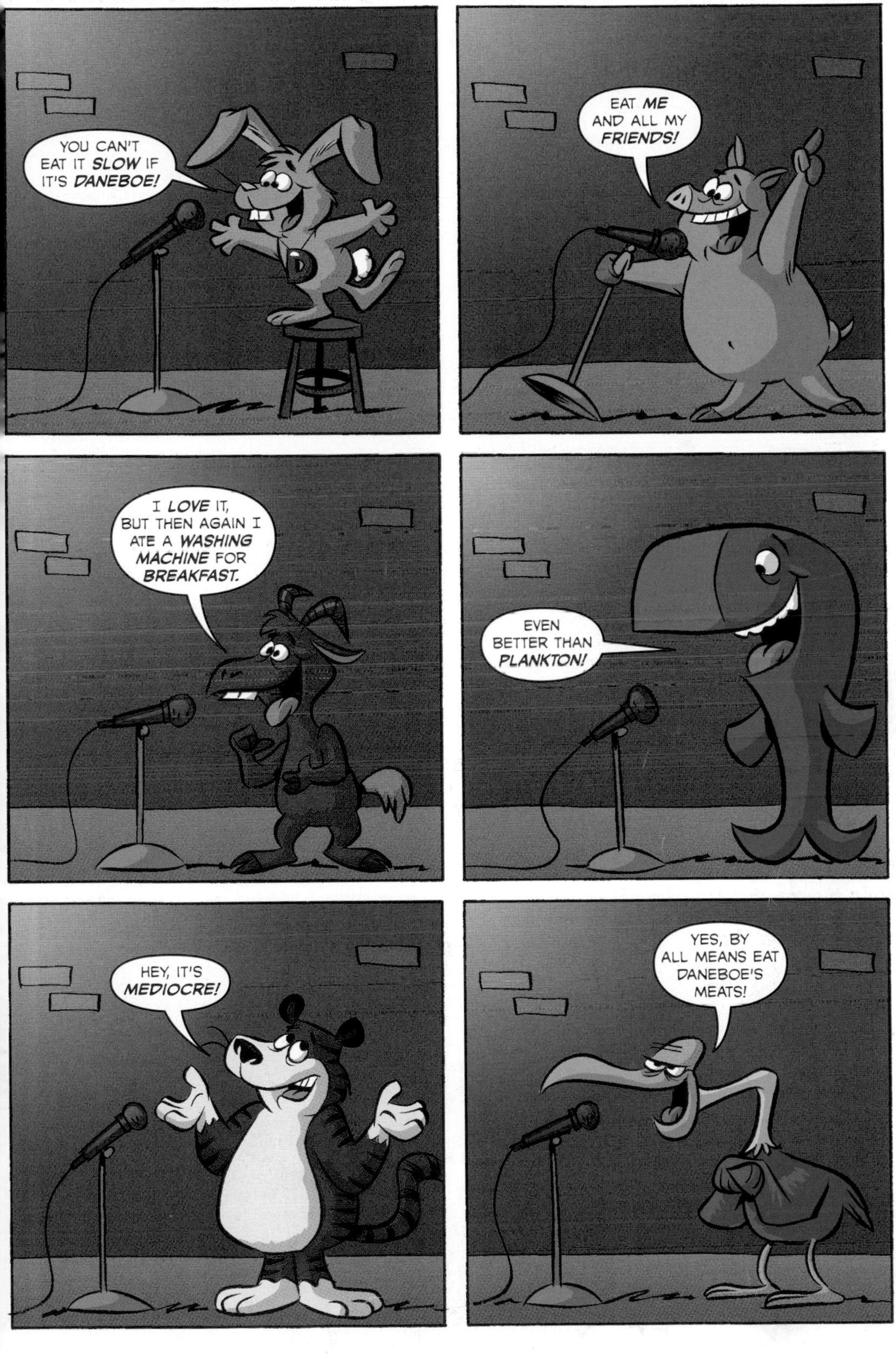
YOU CAN'T EAT IT SLOW IF IT'S DANEBOE!
EAT ME AND ALL MY FRIENDS!
I LOVE IT, BUT THEN AGAIN I ATE A WASHING MACHINE FOR BREAKFAST.
EVEN BETTER THAN PLANKTON!
HEY, IT'S MEDIOCRE!
YES, BY ALL MEANS EAT DANEBOE'S MEATS!

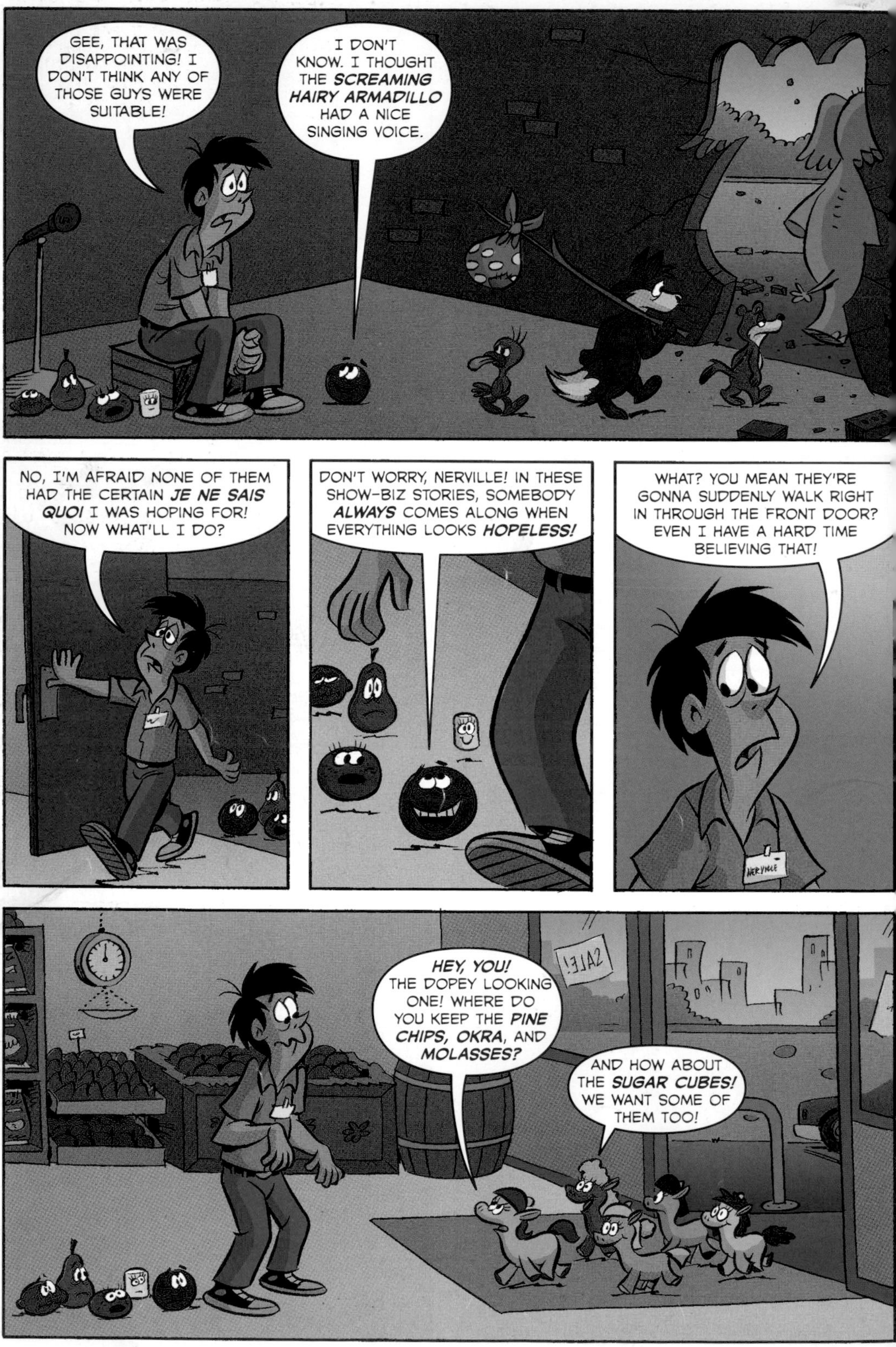
GEE, THAT WAS DISAPPOINTING! I DON'T THINK ANY OF THOSE GUYS WERE SUITABLE!
I DON'T KNOW. I THOUGHT THE SCREAMING HAIRY ARMADILLO HAD A NICE SINGING VOICE.
NO, I'M AFRAID NONE OF THEM HAD THE CERTAIN JE NE SAIS QUOI I WAS HOPING FOR! NOW WHAT'LL I DO?
DON'T WORRY, NERVILLE! IN THESE SHOW-BIZ STORIES, SOMEBODY ALWAYS COMES ALONG WHEN EVERYTHING LOOKS HOPELESS!
WHAT? YOU MEAN THEY'RE GONNA SUDDENLY WALK RIGHT IN THROUGH THE FRONT DOOR? EVEN I HAVE A HARD TIME BELIEVING THAT!
HEY, YOU! THE DOPEY LOOKING ONE! WHERE DO YOU KEEP THE PINE CHIPS, OKRA, AND MOLASSES?
AND HOW ABOUT THE SUGAR CUBES! WE WANT SOME OF THEM TOO!

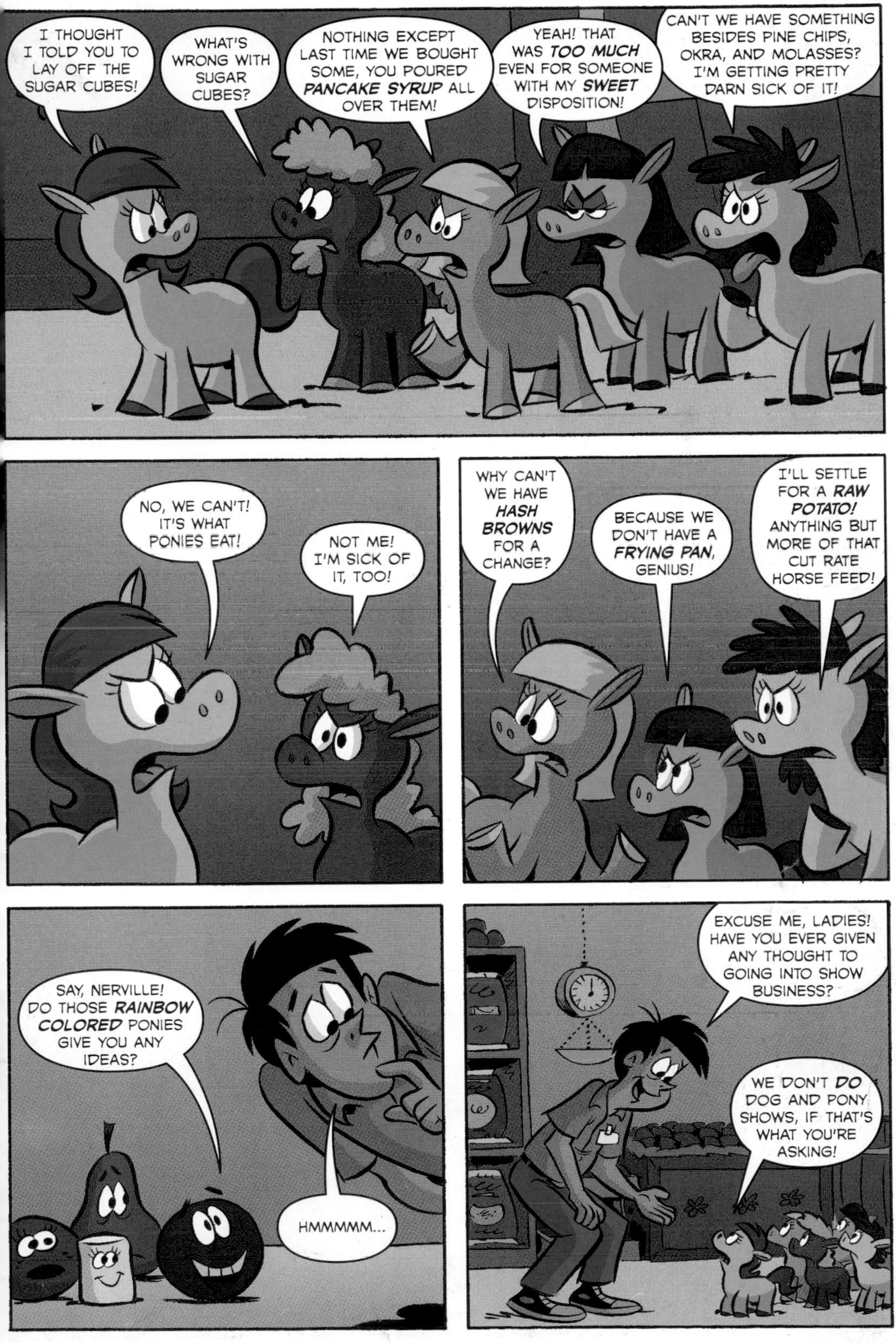
I THOUGHT I TOLD YOU TO LAY OFF THE SUGAR CUBES!
WHAT'S WRONG WITH SUGAR CUBES?
NOTHING EXCEPT LAST TIME WE BOUGHT SOME, YOU POURED PANCAKE SYRUP ALL OVER THEM!
YEAH! THAT WAS TOO MUCH EVEN FOR SOMEONE WITH MY SWEET DISPOSITION!
CAN'T WE HAVE SOMETHING BESIDES PINE CHIPS, OKRA, AND MOLASSES? I'M GETTING PRETTY DARN SICK OF IT!
NO, WE CAN'T! IT'S WHAT PONIES EAT!
NOT ME! I'M SICK OF IT, TOO!
WHY CAN'T WE HAVE HASH BROWNS FOR A CHANGE?
BECAUSE WE DON'T HAVE A FRYING PAN, GENIUS!
I'LL SETTLE FOR A RAW POTATO! ANYTHING BUT MORE OF THAT CUT RATE HORSE FEED!
SAY, NERVILLE! DO THOSE RAINBOW COLORED PONIES GIVE YOU ANY IDEAS?
HMMMMM...
EXCUSE ME, LADIES! HAVE YOU EVER GIVEN ANY THOUGHT TO GOING INTO SHOW BUSINESS?
WE DON'T DO DOG AND PONY SHOWS, IF THAT'S WHAT YOU'RE ASKING!

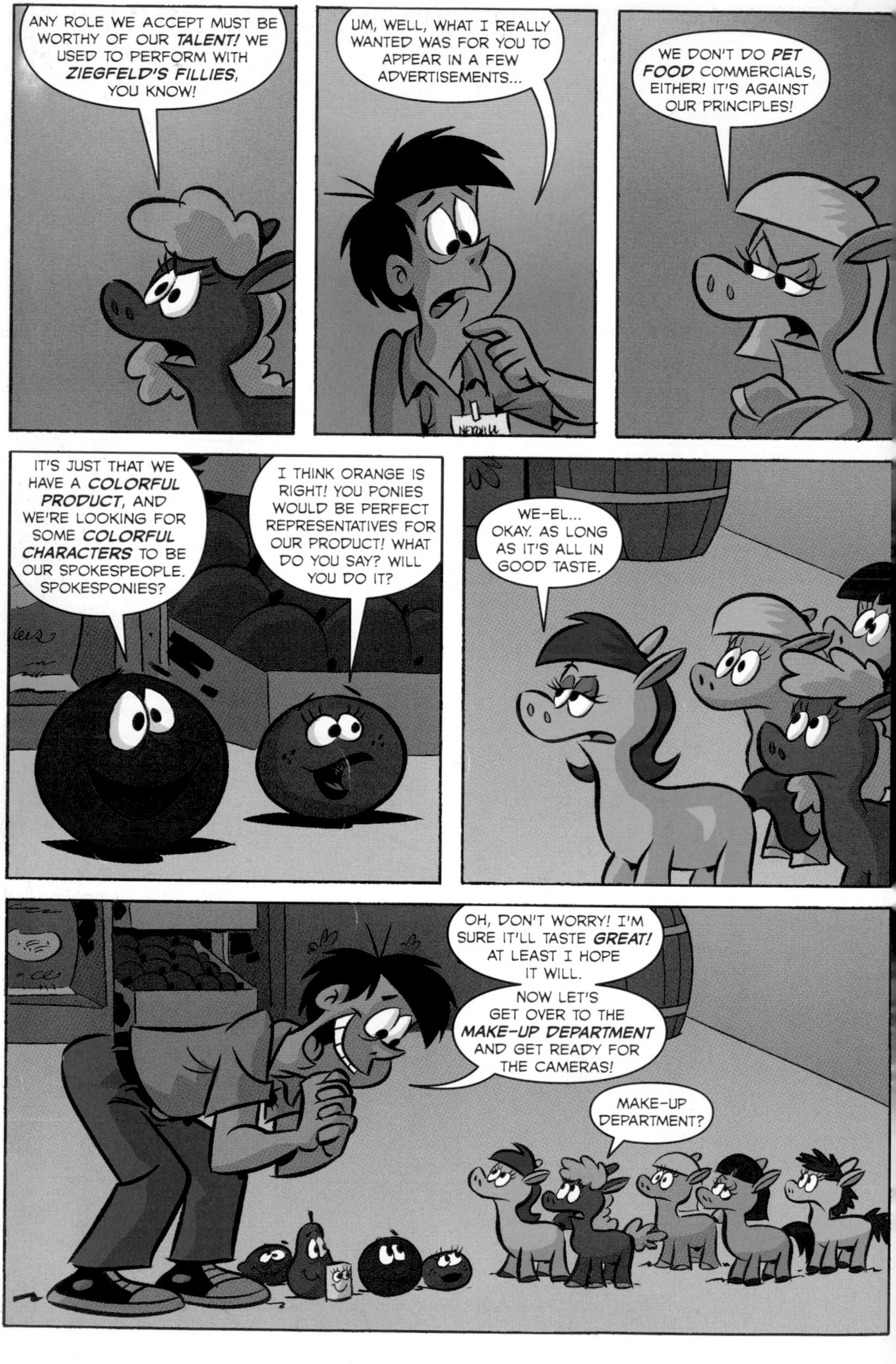
ANY ROLE WE ACCEPT MUST BE WORTHY OF OUR TALENT! WE USED TO PERFORM WITH ZIEGFELD'S FILLIES, YOU KNOW!
UM, WELL, WHAT I REALLY WANTED WAS FOR YOU TO APPEAR IN A FEW ADVERTISEMENTS...
WE DON'T DO PET FOOD COMMERCIALS, EITHER! IT'S AGAINST OUR PRINCIPLES!
IT'S JUST THAT WE HAVE A COLORFUL PRODUCT, AND WE'RE LOOKING FOR SOME COLORFUL CHARACTERS TO BE OUR SPOKESPEOPLE. SPOKESPONIES?
I THINK ORANGE IS RIGHT! YOU PONIES WOULD BE PERFECT REPRESENTATIVES FOR OUR PRODUCT! WHAT DO YOU SAY? WILL YOU DO IT?
WE-EL... OKAY. AS LONG AS IT'S ALL IN GOOD TASTE.
OH, DON'T WORRY! I'M SURE IT'LL TASTE GREAT! AT LEAST I HOPE IT WILL.
NOW LET'S GET OVER TO THE MAKE-UP DEPARTMENT AND GET READY FOR THE CAMERAS!
MAKE-UP DEPARTMENT?

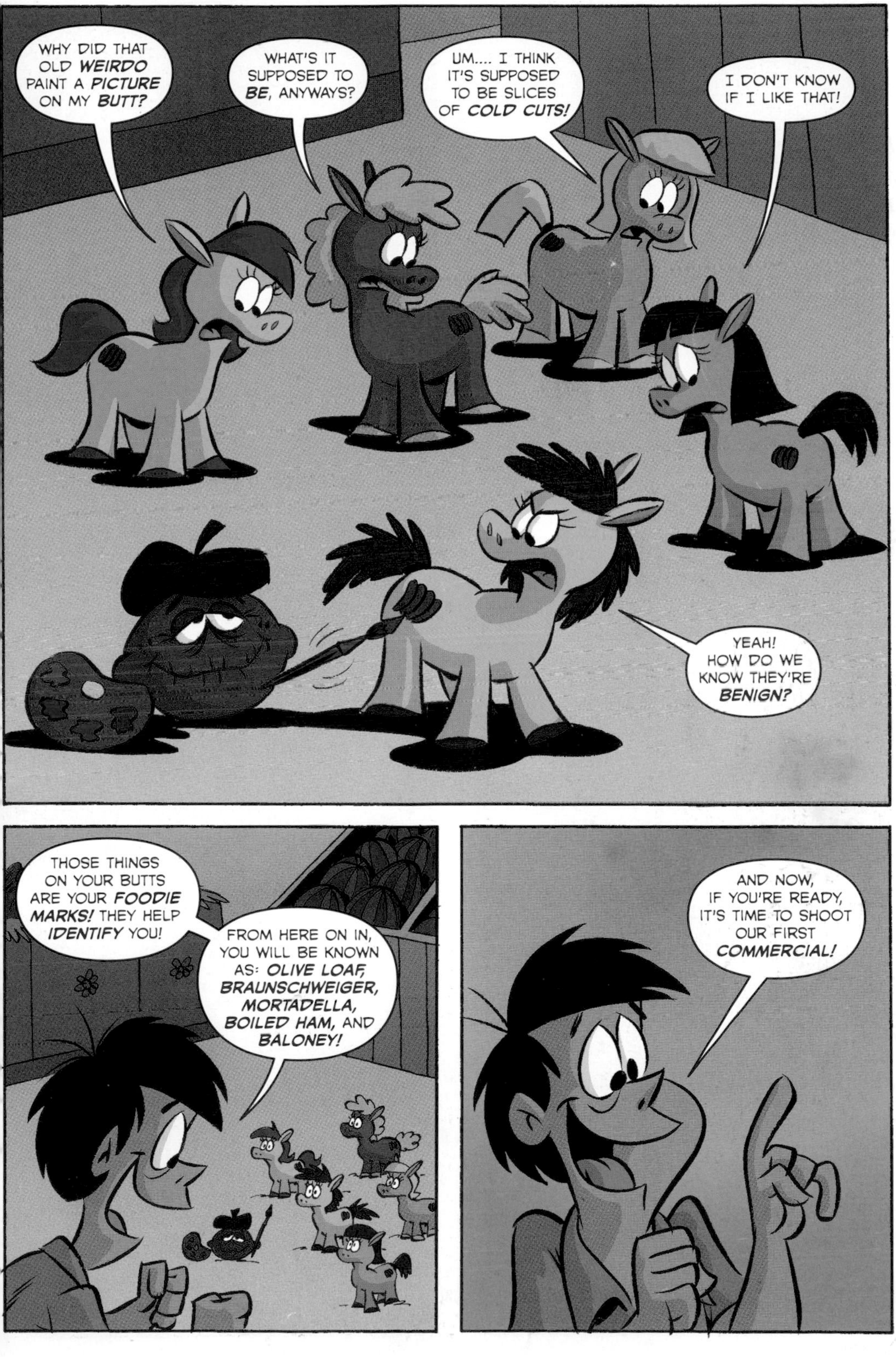
WHY DID THAT OLD *WEIRDO* PAINT A *PICTURE* ON MY *BUTT?*
WHAT'S IT SUPPOSED TO *BE*, ANYWAYS?
UM.... I THINK IT'S SUPPOSED TO BE SLICES OF *COLD CUTS!*
I DON'T KNOW IF I LIKE THAT!
YEAH! HOW DO WE KNOW THEY'RE *BENIGN?*
THOSE THINGS ON YOUR BUTTS ARE YOUR *FOODIE MARKS!* THEY HELP *IDENTIFY* YOU!
FROM HERE ON IN, YOU WILL BE KNOWN AS: *OLIVE LOAF, BRAUNSCHWEIGER, MORTADELLA, BOILED HAM,* AND *BALONEY!*
AND NOW, IF YOU'RE READY, IT'S TIME TO SHOOT OUR FIRST *COMMERCIAL!*

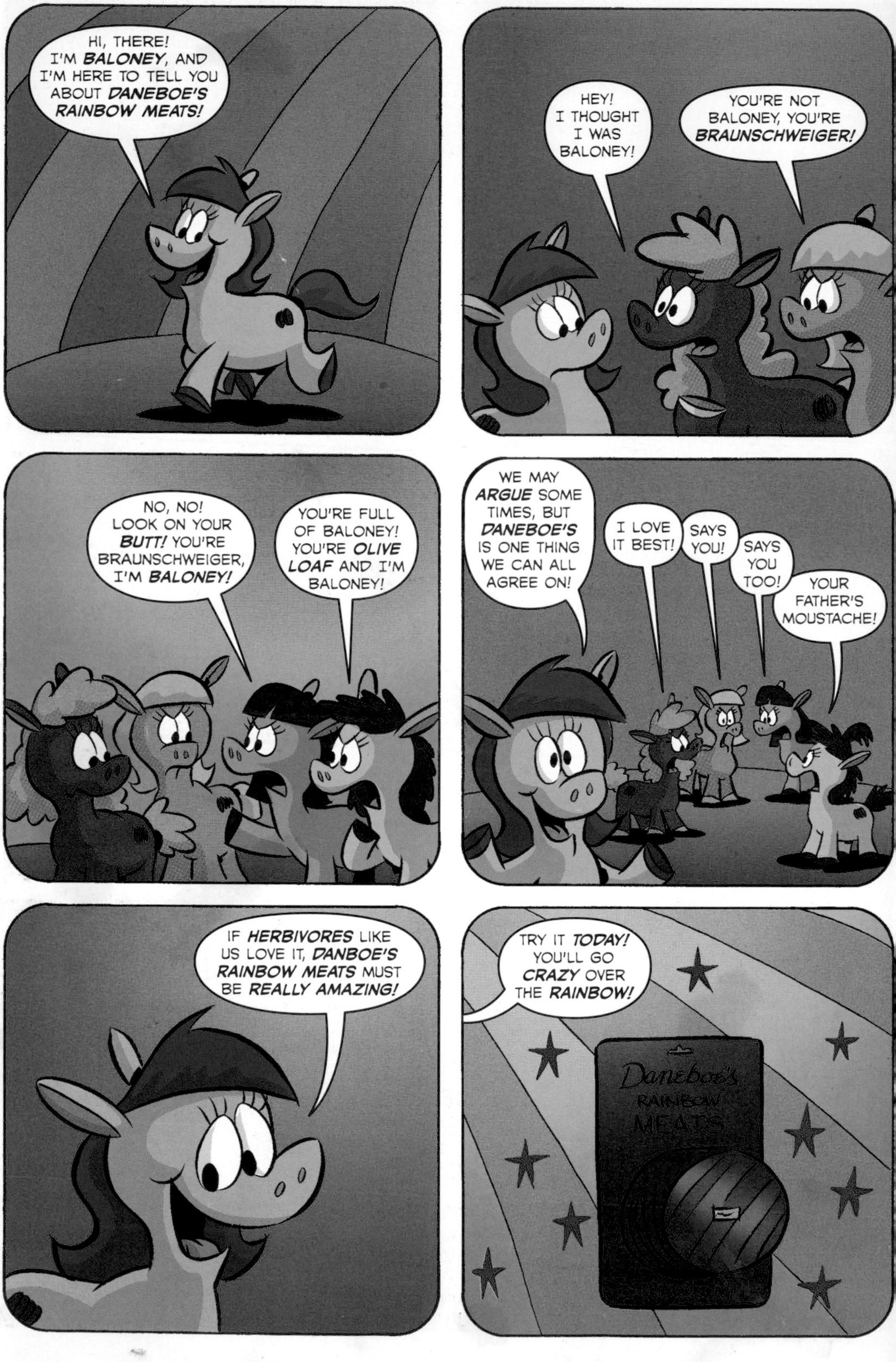
HI, THERE! I'M BALONEY, AND I'M HERE TO TELL YOU ABOUT DANEBOE'S RAINBOW MEATS!
HEY! I THOUGHT I WAS BALONEY!
YOU'RE NOT BALONEY, YOU'RE BRAUNSCHWEIGER!
NO, NO! LOOK ON YOUR BUTT! YOU'RE BRAUNSCHWEIGER, I'M BALONEY!
YOU'RE FULL OF BALONEY! YOU'RE OLIVE LOAF AND I'M BALONEY!
WE MAY ARGUE SOMETIMES, BUT DANEBOE'S IS ONE THING WE CAN ALL AGREE ON!
I LOVE IT BEST!
SAYS YOU!
SAYS YOU TOO!
YOUR FATHER'S MOUSTACHE!
IF HERBIVORES LIKE US LOVE IT, DANBOE'S RAINBOW MEATS MUST BE REALLY AMAZING!
TRY IT TODAY! YOU'LL GO CRAZY OVER THE RAINBOW!
Daneboe's
RAINBOW
MEATS

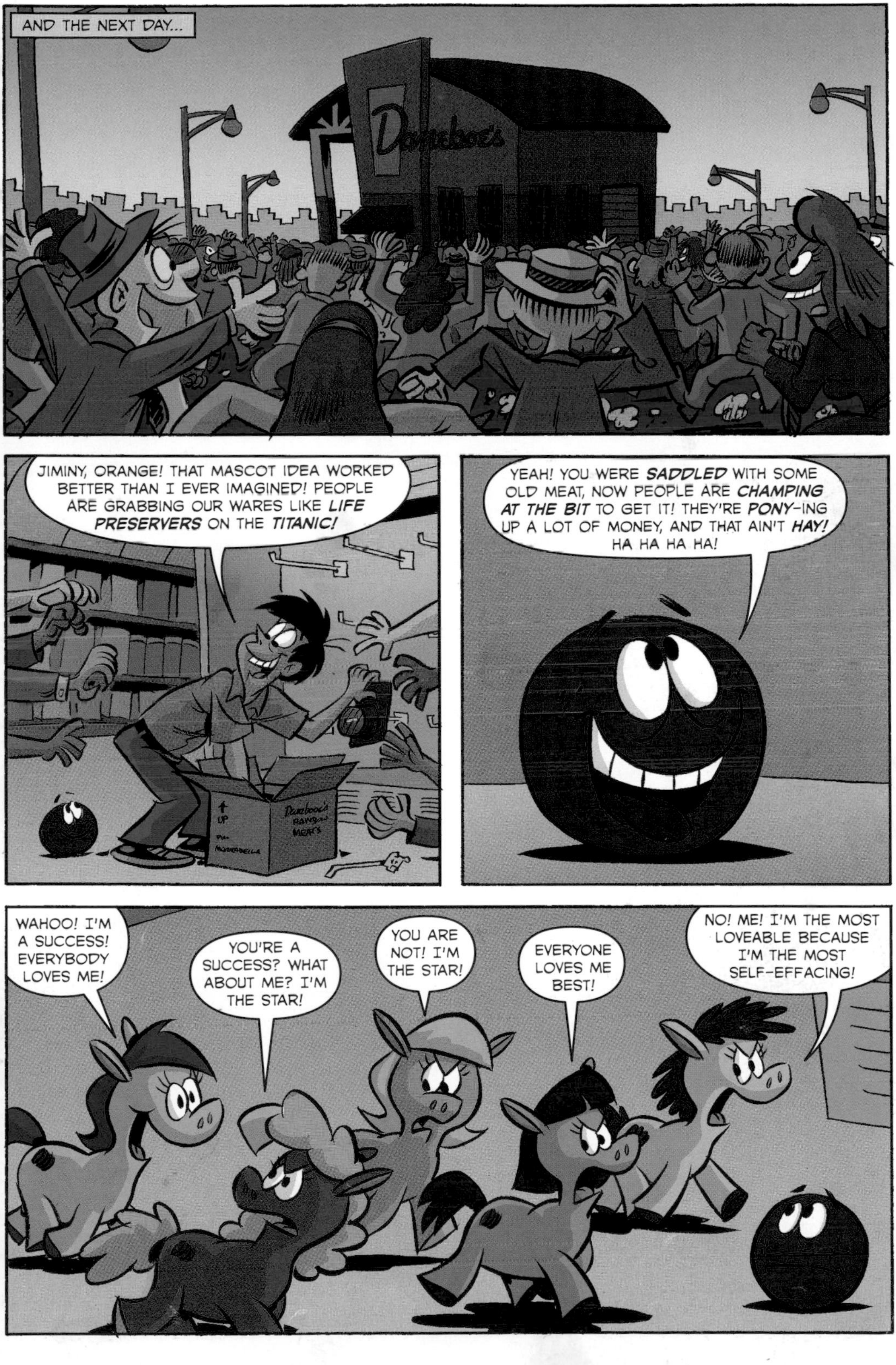
AND THE NEXT DAY...
JIMINY, ORANGE! THAT MASCOT IDEA WORKED BETTER THAN I EVER IMAGINED! PEOPLE ARE GRABBING OUR WARES LIKE *LIFE PRESERVERS* ON THE *TITANIC!*
YEAH! YOU WERE ***SADDLED*** WITH SOME OLD MEAT, NOW PEOPLE ARE ***CHAMPING AT THE BIT*** TO GET IT! THEY'RE ***PONY***-ING UP A LOT OF MONEY, AND THAT AIN'T ***HAY!*** HA HA HA HA!
WAHOO! I'M A SUCCESS! EVERYBODY LOVES ME!
YOU'RE A SUCCESS? WHAT ABOUT ME? I'M THE STAR!
YOU ARE NOT! I'M THE STAR!
EVERYONE LOVES ME BEST!
NO! ME! I'M THE MOST LOVEABLE BECAUSE I'M THE MOST SELF-EFFACING!

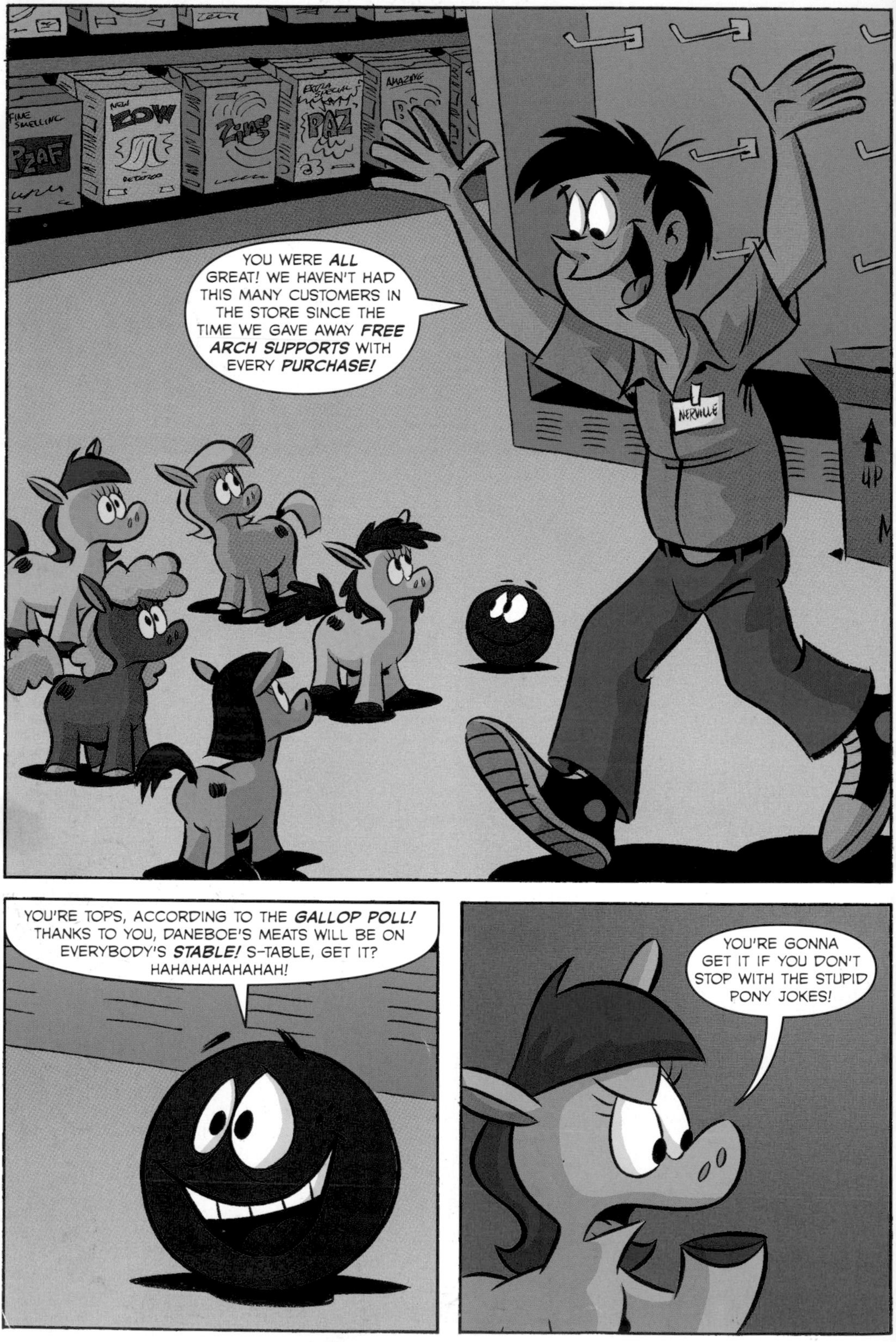
YOU WERE ALL GREAT! WE HAVEN'T HAD THIS MANY CUSTOMERS IN THE STORE SINCE THE TIME WE GAVE AWAY FREE ARCH SUPPORTS WITH EVERY PURCHASE!
NERVILLE
YOU'RE TOPS, ACCORDING TO THE GALLOP POLL! THANKS TO YOU, DANEBOE'S MEATS WILL BE ON EVERYBODY'S STABLE! S-TABLE, GET IT? HAHAHAHAHAHAH!
YOU'RE GONNA GET IT IF YOU DON'T STOP WITH THE STUPID PONY JOKES!

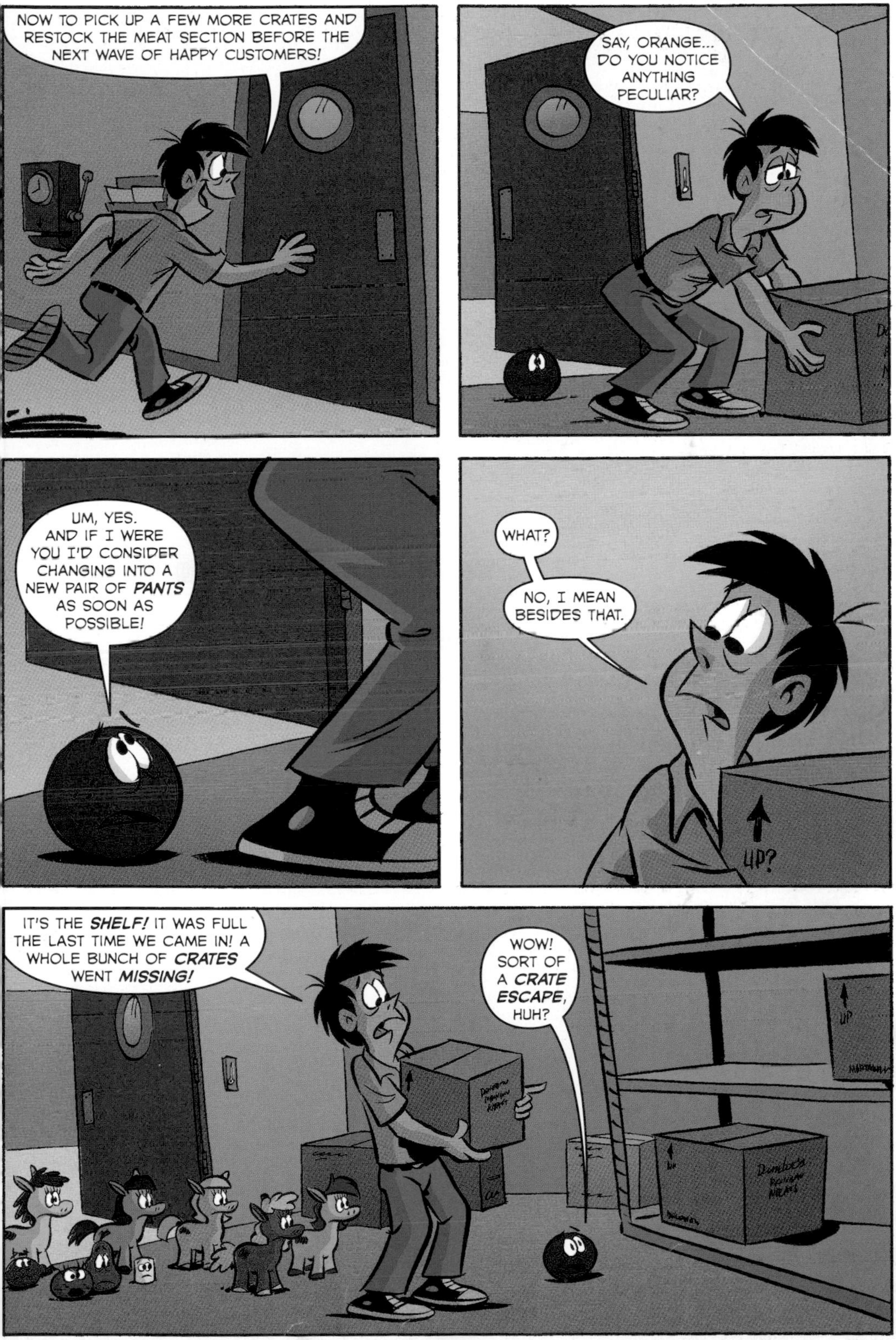

NOW TO PICK UP A FEW MORE CRATES AND RESTOCK THE MEAT SECTION BEFORE THE NEXT WAVE OF HAPPY CUSTOMERS!
SAY, ORANGE... DO YOU NOTICE ANYTHING PECULIAR?
UM, YES. AND IF I WERE YOU I'D CONSIDER CHANGING INTO A NEW PAIR OF *PANTS* AS SOON AS POSSIBLE!
WHAT?
NO, I MEAN BESIDES THAT.
UP?
IT'S THE *SHELF!* IT WAS FULL THE LAST TIME WE CAME IN! A WHOLE BUNCH OF *CRATES* WENT *MISSING!*
WOW! SORT OF A *CRATE ESCAPE*, HUH?
UP

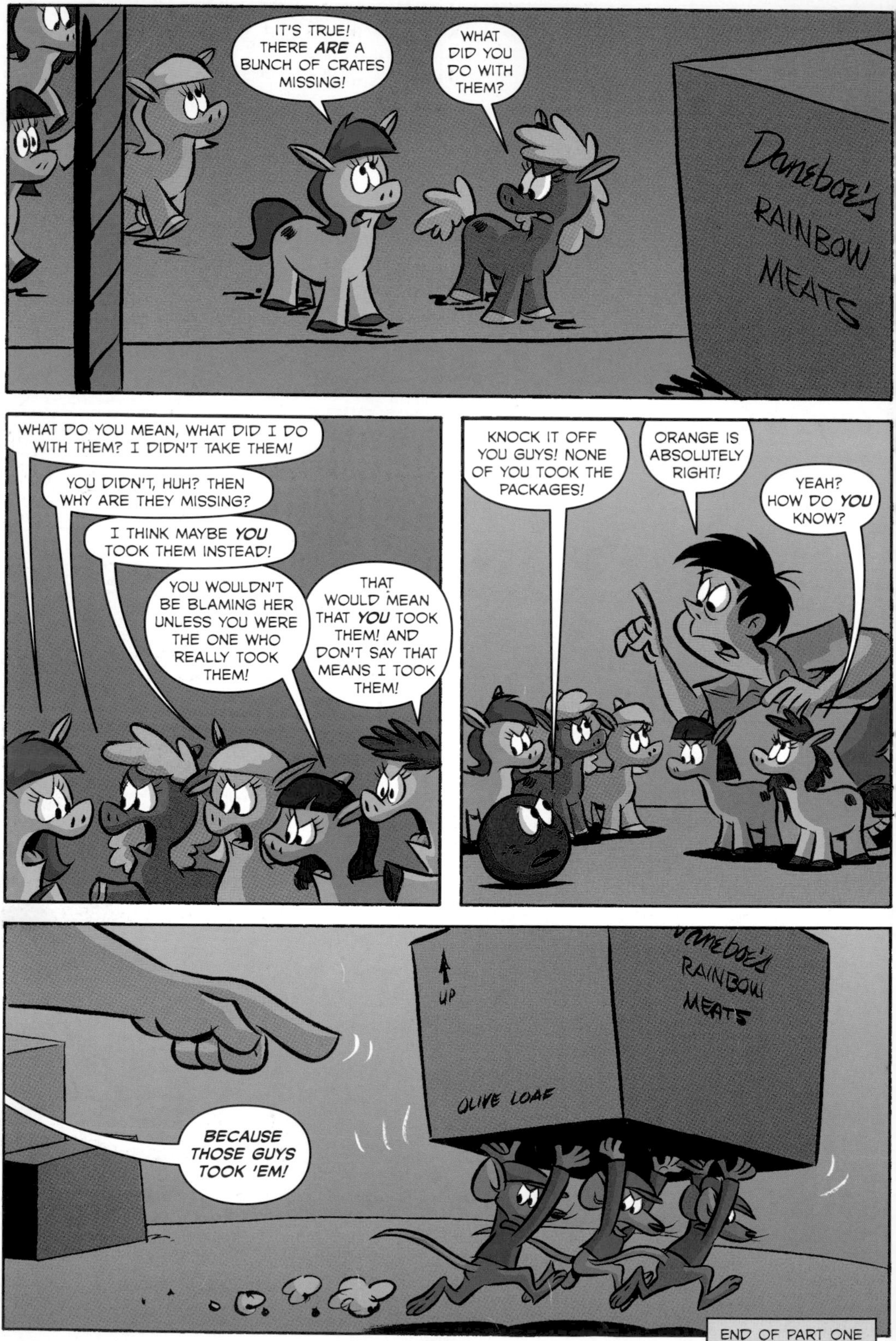
IT'S TRUE! THERE ARE A BUNCH OF CRATES MISSING!
WHAT DID YOU DO WITH THEM?
Danebo's RAINBOW MEATS
WHAT DO YOU MEAN, WHAT DID I DO WITH THEM? I DIDN'T TAKE THEM!
YOU DIDN'T, HUH? THEN WHY ARE THEY MISSING?
I THINK MAYBE YOU TOOK THEM INSTEAD!
YOU WOULDN'T BE BLAMING HER UNLESS YOU WERE THE ONE WHO REALLY TOOK THEM!
THAT WOULD MEAN THAT YOU TOOK THEM! AND DON'T SAY THAT MEANS I TOOK THEM!
KNOCK IT OFF YOU GUYS! NONE OF YOU TOOK THE PACKAGES!
ORANGE IS ABSOLUTELY RIGHT!
YEAH? HOW DO YOU KNOW?
UP
Danebo's RAINBOW MEATS
OLIVE LOAF
BECAUSE THOSE GUYS TOOK 'EM!
END OF PART ONE

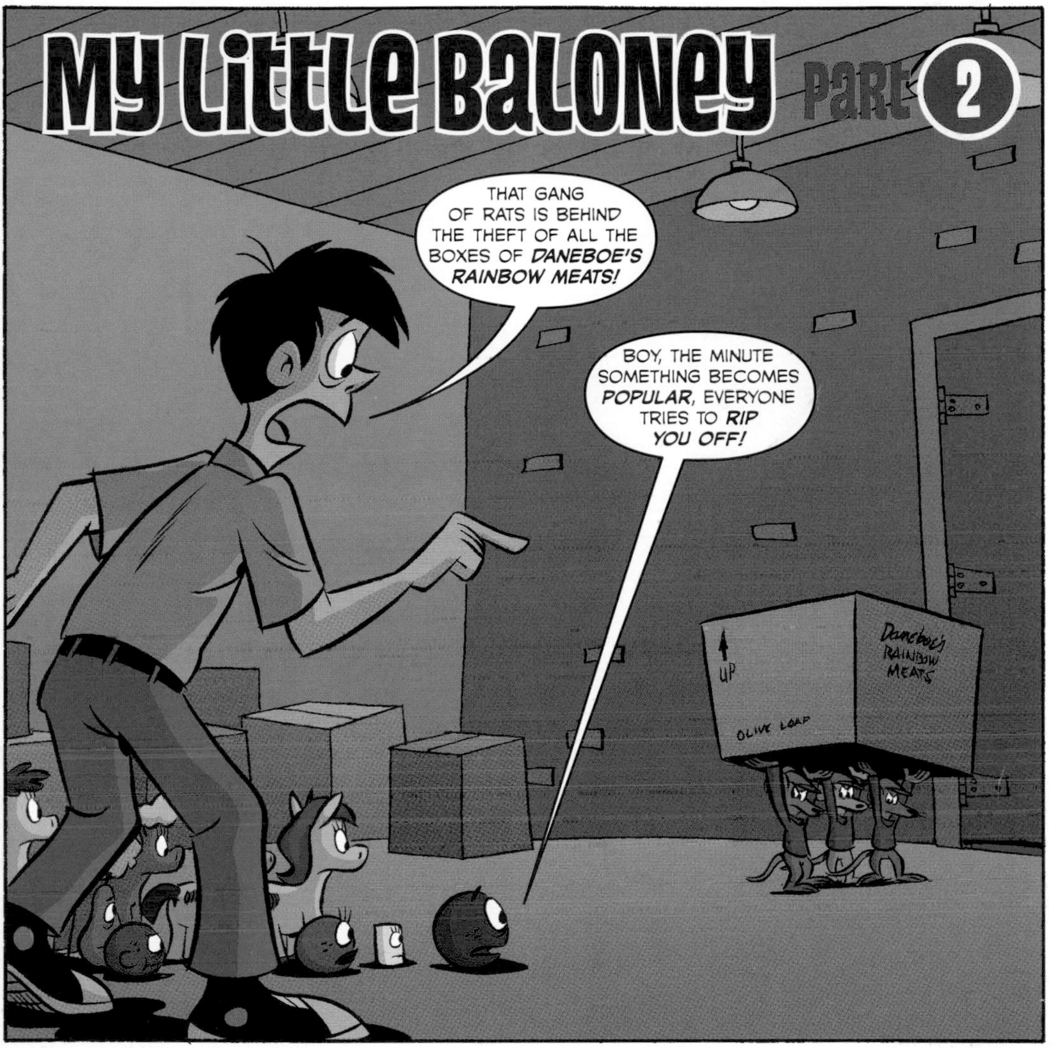
My Little Baloney Part 2
THAT GANG OF RATS IS BEHIND THE THEFT OF ALL THE BOXES OF *DANEBOE'S RAINBOW MEATS!*
BOY, THE MINUTE SOMETHING BECOMES *POPULAR*, EVERYONE TRIES TO *RIP YOU OFF!*
UP
Daneboe's RAINBOW MEATS
OLIVE LOAF

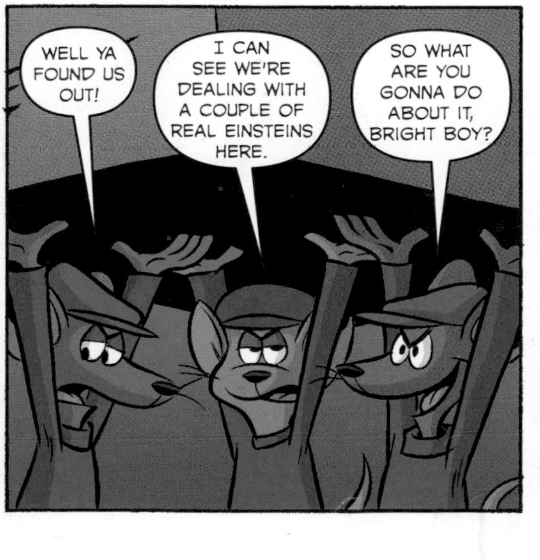
WELL YA FOUND US OUT!
I CAN SEE WE'RE DEALING WITH A COUPLE OF REAL EINSTEINS HERE.
SO WHAT ARE YOU GONNA DO ABOUT IT, BRIGHT BOY?

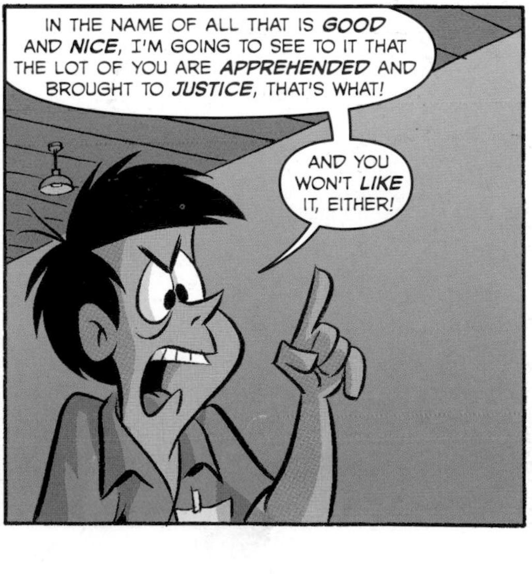
IN THE NAME OF ALL THAT IS *GOOD* AND *NICE*, I'M GOING TO SEE TO IT THAT THE LOT OF YOU ARE *APPREHENDED* AND BROUGHT TO *JUSTICE*, THAT'S WHAT!
AND YOU WON'T *LIKE* IT, EITHER!

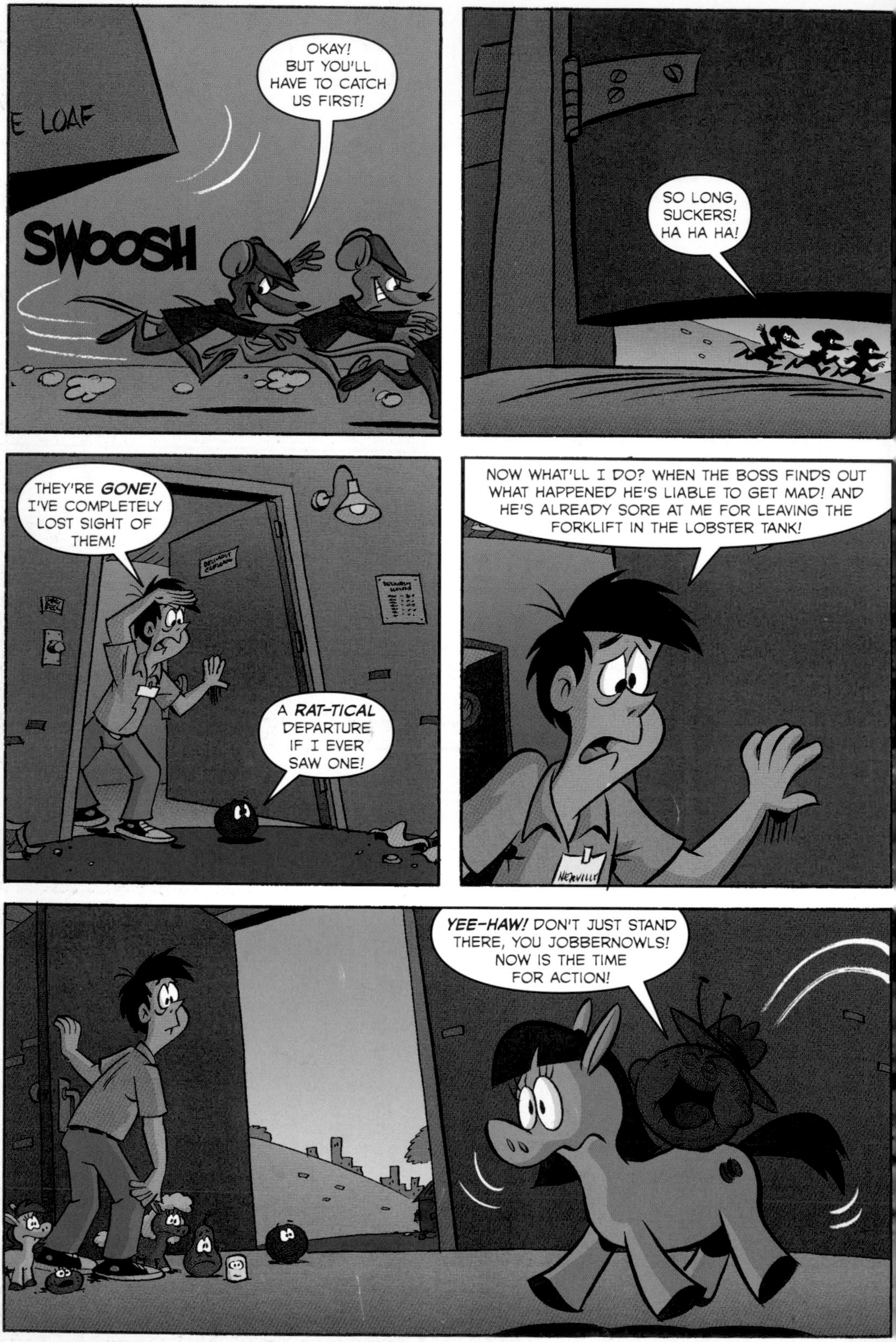
E LOAF
OKAY! BUT YOU'LL HAVE TO CATCH US FIRST!
SWOOSH
SO LONG, SUCKERS! HA HA HA!
THEY'RE GONE! I'VE COMPLETELY LOST SIGHT OF THEM!
A RAT-TICAL DEPARTURE IF I EVER SAW ONE!
NOW WHAT'LL I DO? WHEN THE BOSS FINDS OUT WHAT HAPPENED HE'S LIABLE TO GET MAD! AND HE'S ALREADY SORE AT ME FOR LEAVING THE FORKLIFT IN THE LOBSTER TANK!
YEE-HAW! DON'T JUST STAND THERE, YOU JOBBERNOWLS! NOW IS THE TIME FOR ACTION!

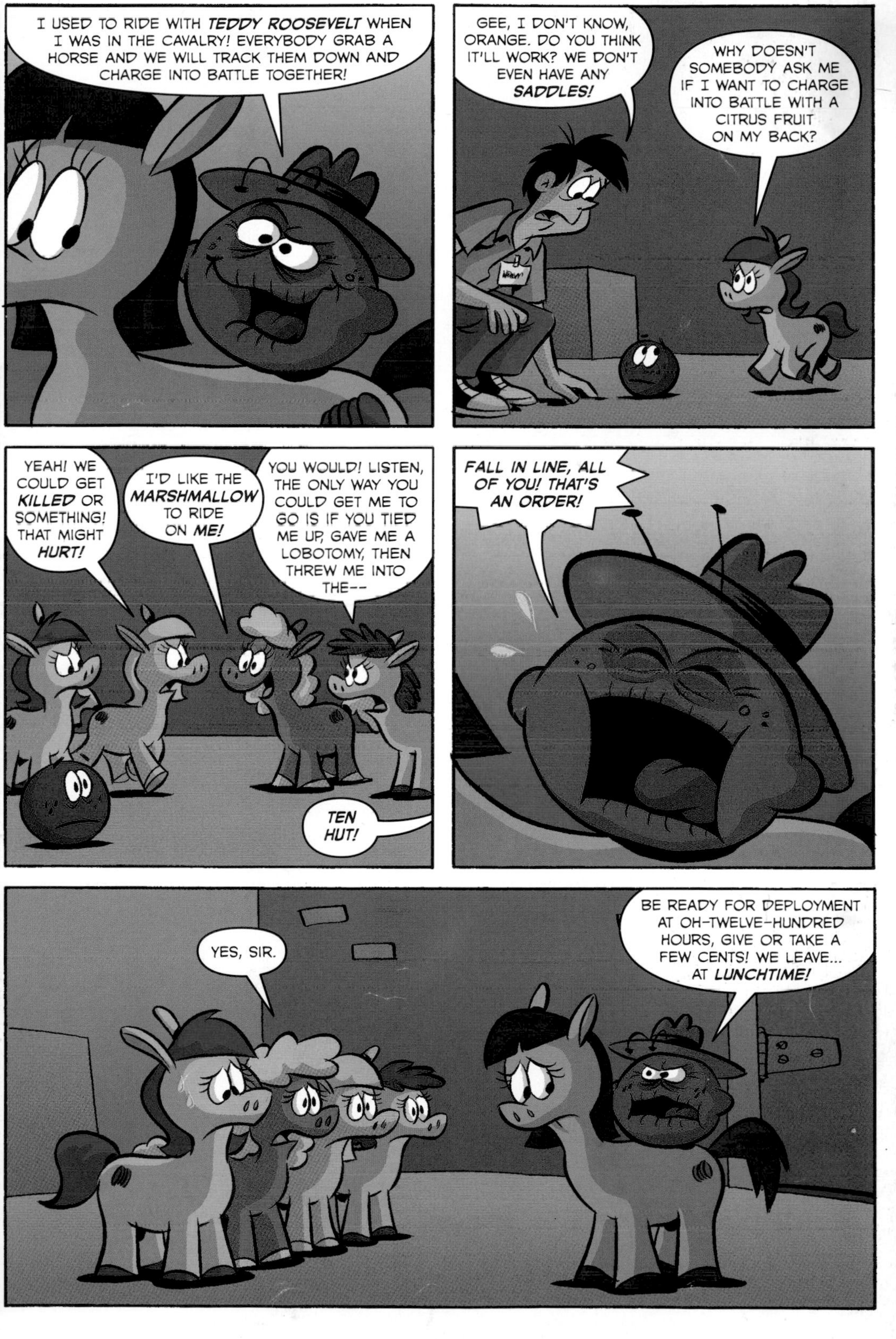

I USED TO RIDE WITH TEDDY ROOSEVELT WHEN I WAS IN THE CAVALRY! EVERYBODY GRAB A HORSE AND WE WILL TRACK THEM DOWN AND CHARGE INTO BATTLE TOGETHER!
GEE, I DON'T KNOW, ORANGE. DO YOU THINK IT'LL WORK? WE DON'T EVEN HAVE ANY SADDLES!
WHY DOESN'T SOMEBODY ASK ME IF I WANT TO CHARGE INTO BATTLE WITH A CITRUS FRUIT ON MY BACK?
YEAH! WE COULD GET KILLED OR SOMETHING! THAT MIGHT HURT!
I'D LIKE THE MARSHMALLOW TO RIDE ON ME!
YOU WOULD! LISTEN, THE ONLY WAY YOU COULD GET ME TO GO IS IF YOU TIED ME UP, GAVE ME A LOBOTOMY, THEN THREW ME INTO THE--
TEN HUT!
FALL IN LINE, ALL OF YOU! THAT'S AN ORDER!
YES, SIR.
BE READY FOR DEPLOYMENT AT OH-TWELVE-HUNDRED HOURS, GIVE OR TAKE A FEW CENTS! WE LEAVE... AT LUNCHTIME!

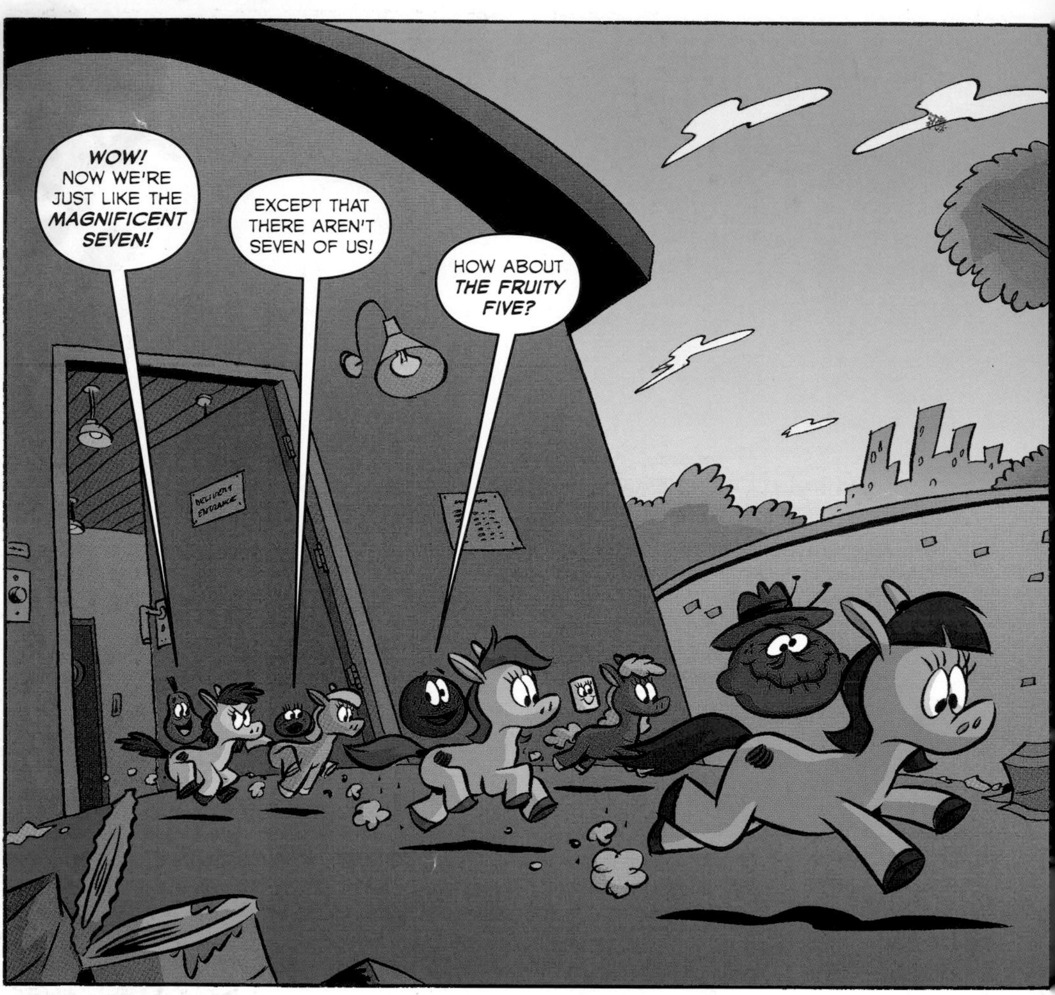
WOW! NOW WE'RE JUST LIKE THE MAGNIFICENT SEVEN!
EXCEPT THAT THERE AREN'T SEVEN OF US!
HOW ABOUT THE FRUITY FIVE?

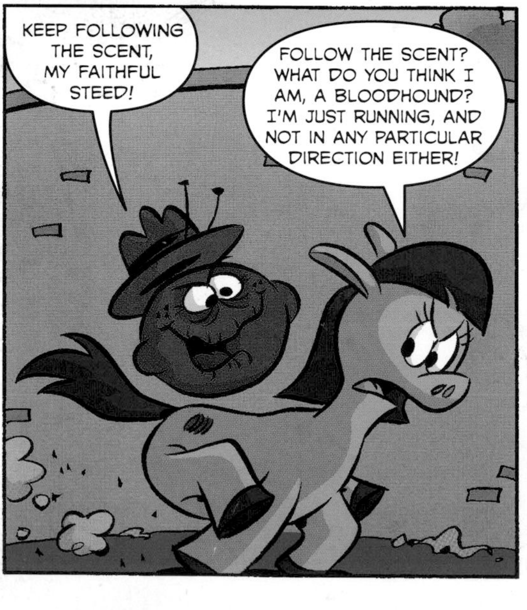
KEEP FOLLOWING THE SCENT, MY FAITHFUL STEED!
FOLLOW THE SCENT? WHAT DO YOU THINK I AM, A BLOODHOUND? I'M JUST RUNNING, AND NOT IN ANY PARTICULAR DIRECTION EITHER!

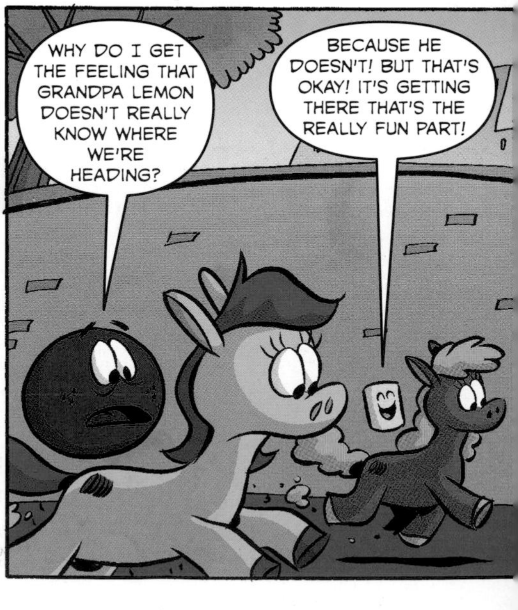
WHY DO I GET THE FEELING THAT GRANDPA LEMON DOESN'T REALLY KNOW WHERE WE'RE HEADING?
BECAUSE HE DOESN'T! BUT THAT'S OKAY! IT'S GETTING THERE THAT'S THE REALLY FUN PART!

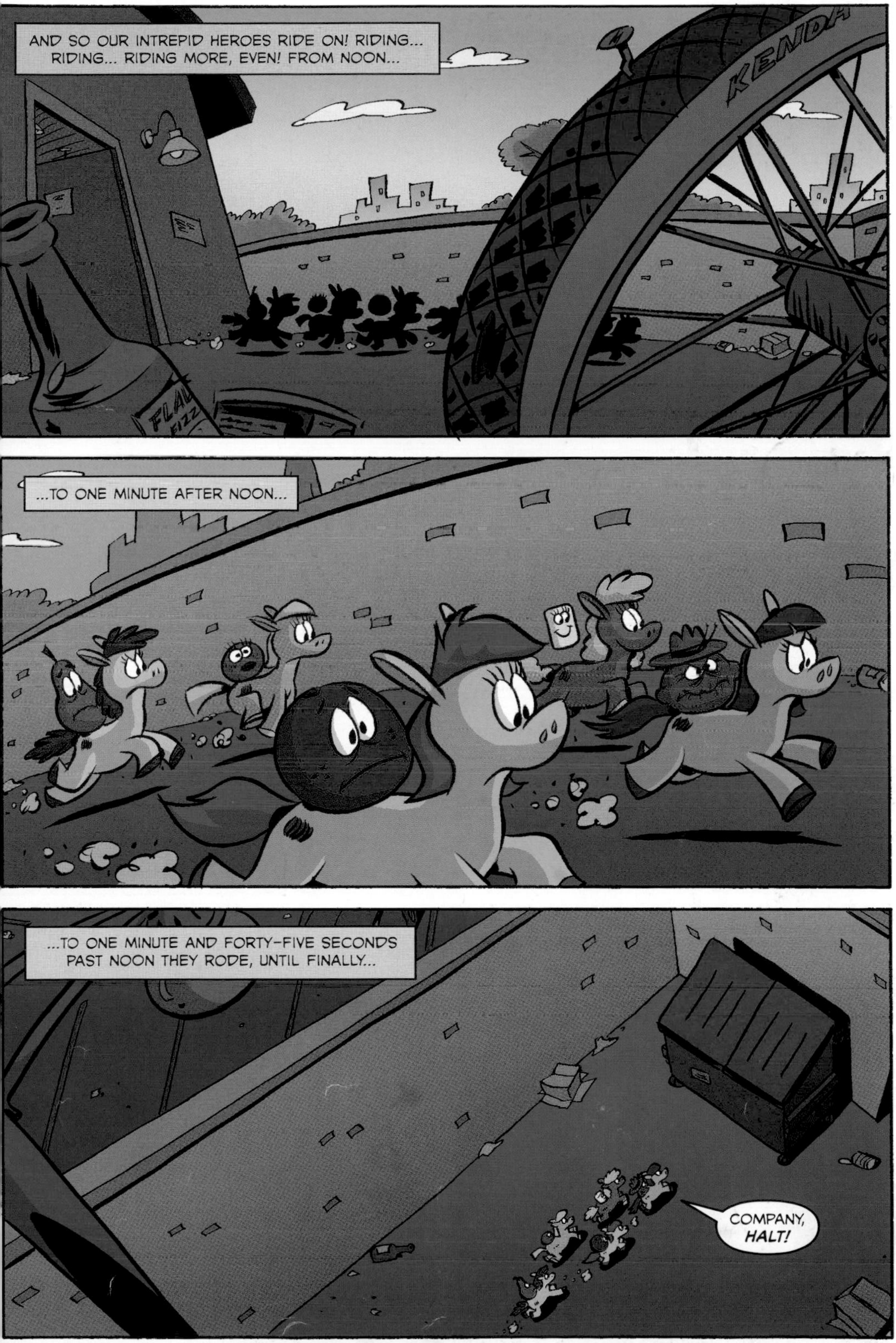
AND SO OUR INTREPID HEROES RIDE ON! RIDING... RIDING... RIDING MORE, EVEN! FROM NOON...
KENDA
...TO ONE MINUTE AFTER NOON...
...TO ONE MINUTE AND FORTY-FIVE SECONDS PAST NOON THEY RODE, UNTIL FINALLY...
COMPANY, *HALT!*

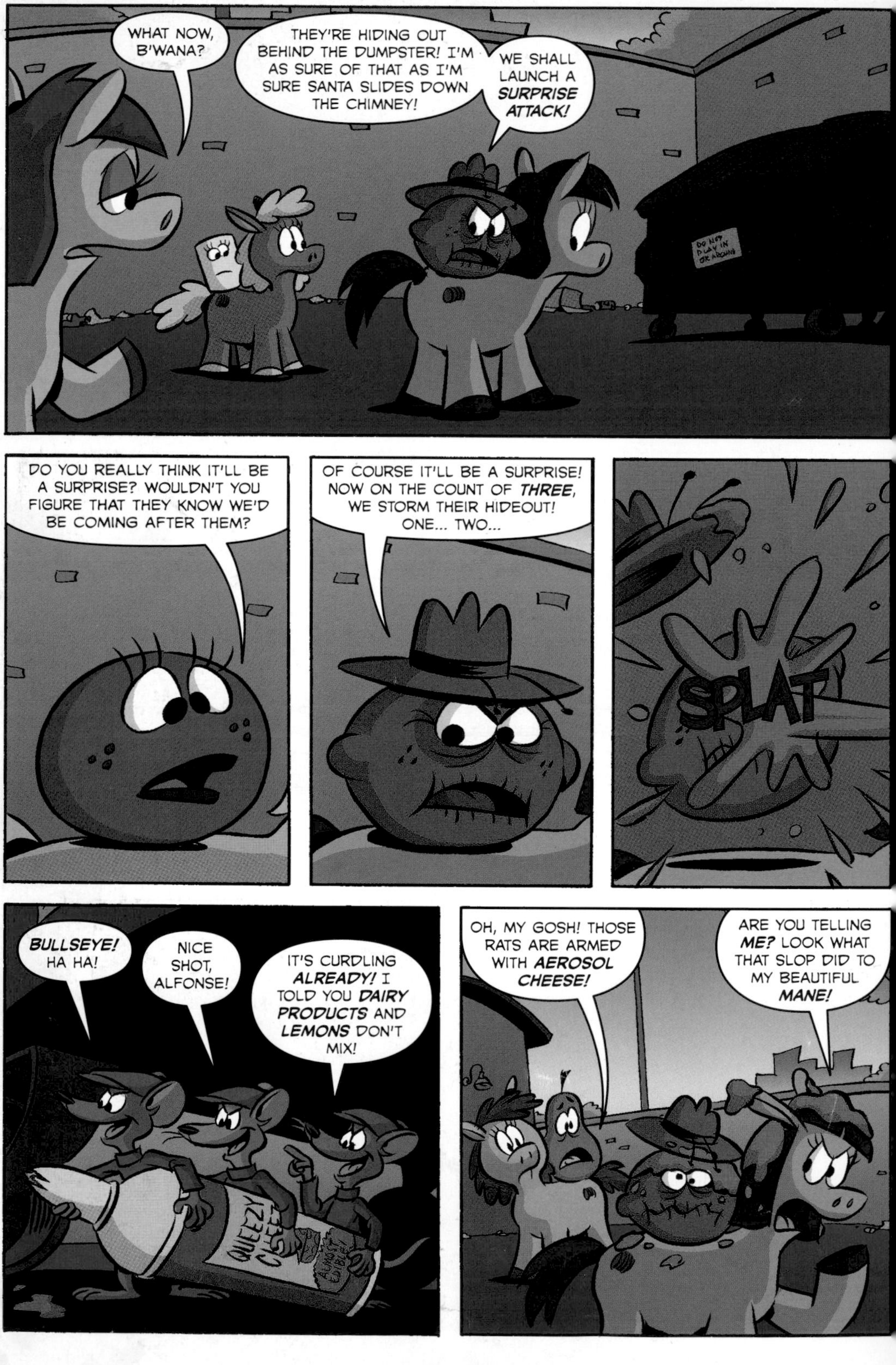
WHAT NOW, B'WANA?
THEY'RE HIDING OUT BEHIND THE DUMPSTER! I'M AS SURE OF THAT AS I'M SURE SANTA SLIDES DOWN THE CHIMNEY!
WE SHALL LAUNCH A SURPRISE ATTACK!
DO YOU REALLY THINK IT'LL BE A SURPRISE? WOULDN'T YOU FIGURE THAT THEY KNOW WE'D BE COMING AFTER THEM?
OF COURSE IT'LL BE A SURPRISE! NOW ON THE COUNT OF THREE, WE STORM THEIR HIDEOUT! ONE... TWO...
SPLAT
BULLSEYE! HA HA!
NICE SHOT, ALFONSE!
IT'S CURDLING ALREADY! I TOLD YOU DAIRY PRODUCTS AND LEMONS DON'T MIX!
OH, MY GOSH! THOSE RATS ARE ARMED WITH AEROSOL CHEESE!
ARE YOU TELLING ME? LOOK WHAT THAT SLOP DID TO MY BEAUTIFUL MANE!

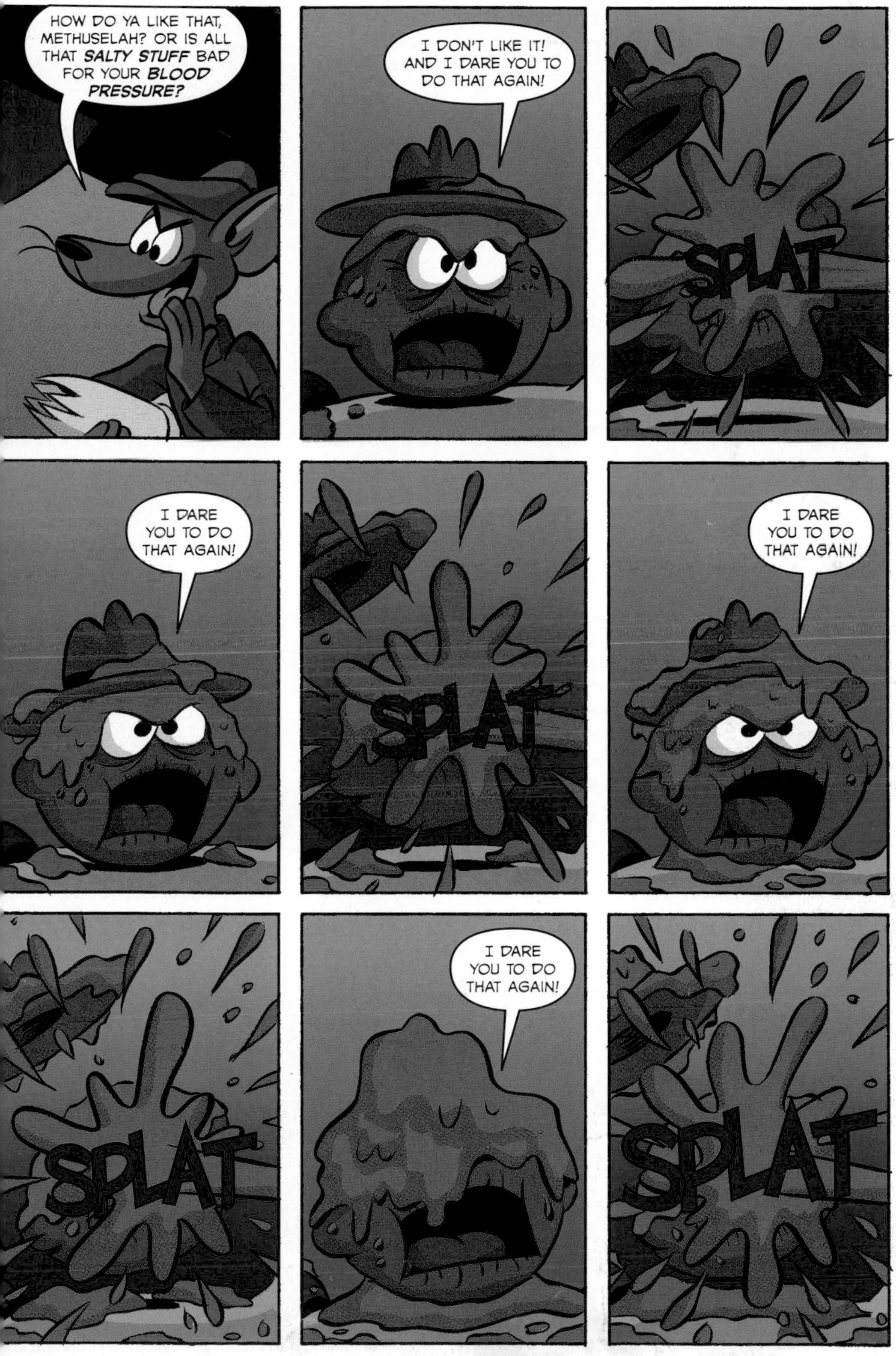
HOW DO YA LIKE THAT, METHUSELAH? OR IS ALL THAT SALTY STUFF BAD FOR YOUR BLOOD PRESSURE?
I DON'T LIKE IT! AND I DARE YOU TO DO THAT AGAIN!
SPLAT
I DARE YOU TO DO THAT AGAIN!
SPLAT
I DARE YOU TO DO THAT AGAIN!
SPLAT
I DARE YOU TO DO THAT AGAIN!
SPLAT

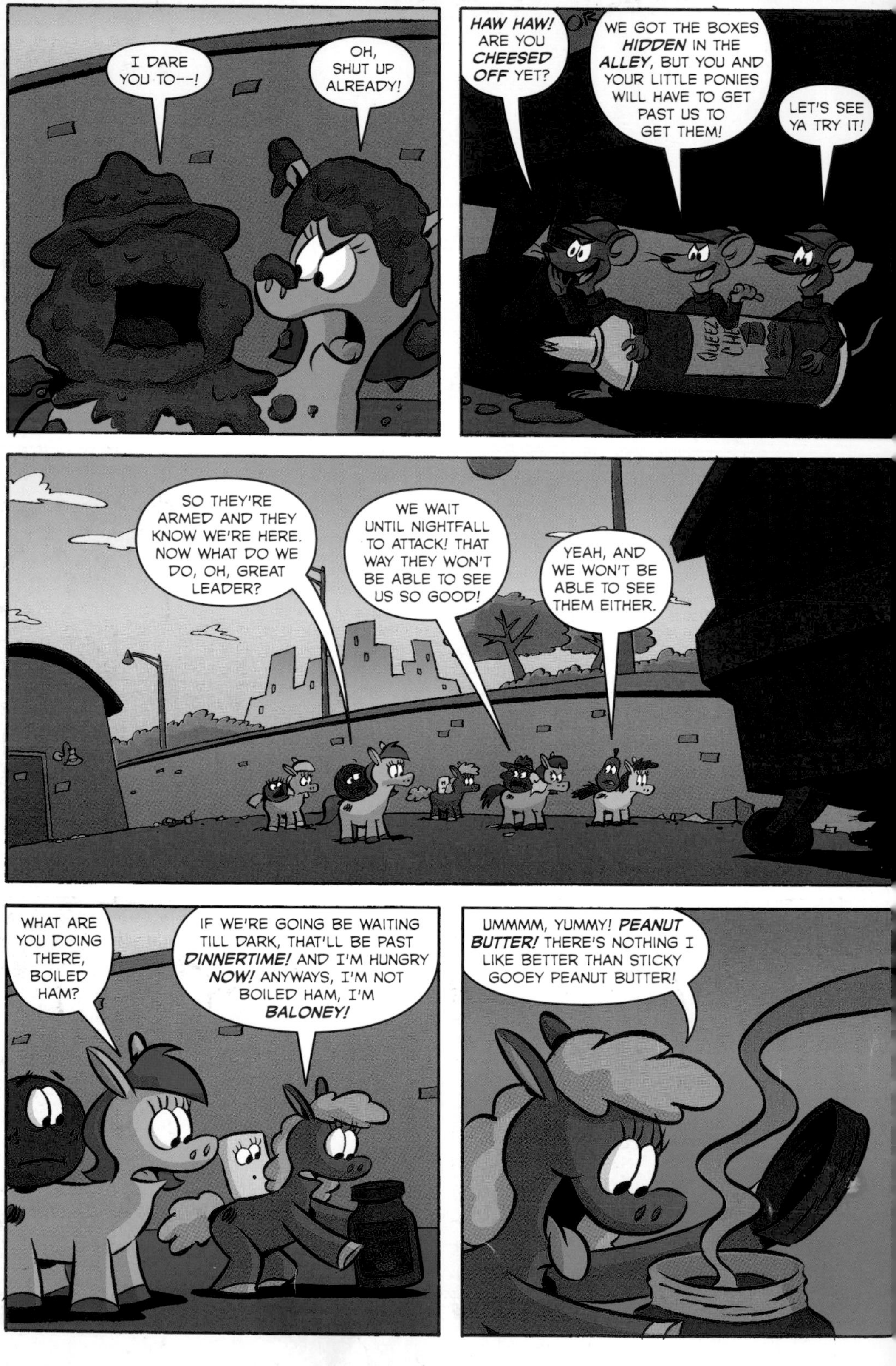
I DARE YOU TO--!
OH, SHUT UP ALREADY!
HAW HAW! ARE YOU CHEESED OFF YET?
WE GOT THE BOXES HIDDEN IN THE ALLEY, BUT YOU AND YOUR LITTLE PONIES WILL HAVE TO GET PAST US TO GET THEM!
LET'S SEE YA TRY IT!
SO THEY'RE ARMED AND THEY KNOW WE'RE HERE. NOW WHAT DO WE DO, OH, GREAT LEADER?
WE WAIT UNTIL NIGHTFALL TO ATTACK! THAT WAY THEY WON'T BE ABLE TO SEE US SO GOOD!
YEAH, AND WE WON'T BE ABLE TO SEE THEM EITHER.
WHAT ARE YOU DOING THERE, BOILED HAM?
IF WE'RE GOING BE WAITING TILL DARK, THAT'LL BE PAST DINNERTIME! AND I'M HUNGRY NOW! ANYWAYS, I'M NOT BOILED HAM, I'M BALONEY!
UMMMM, YUMMY! PEANUT BUTTER! THERE'S NOTHING I LIKE BETTER THAN STICKY GOOEY PEANUT BUTTER!

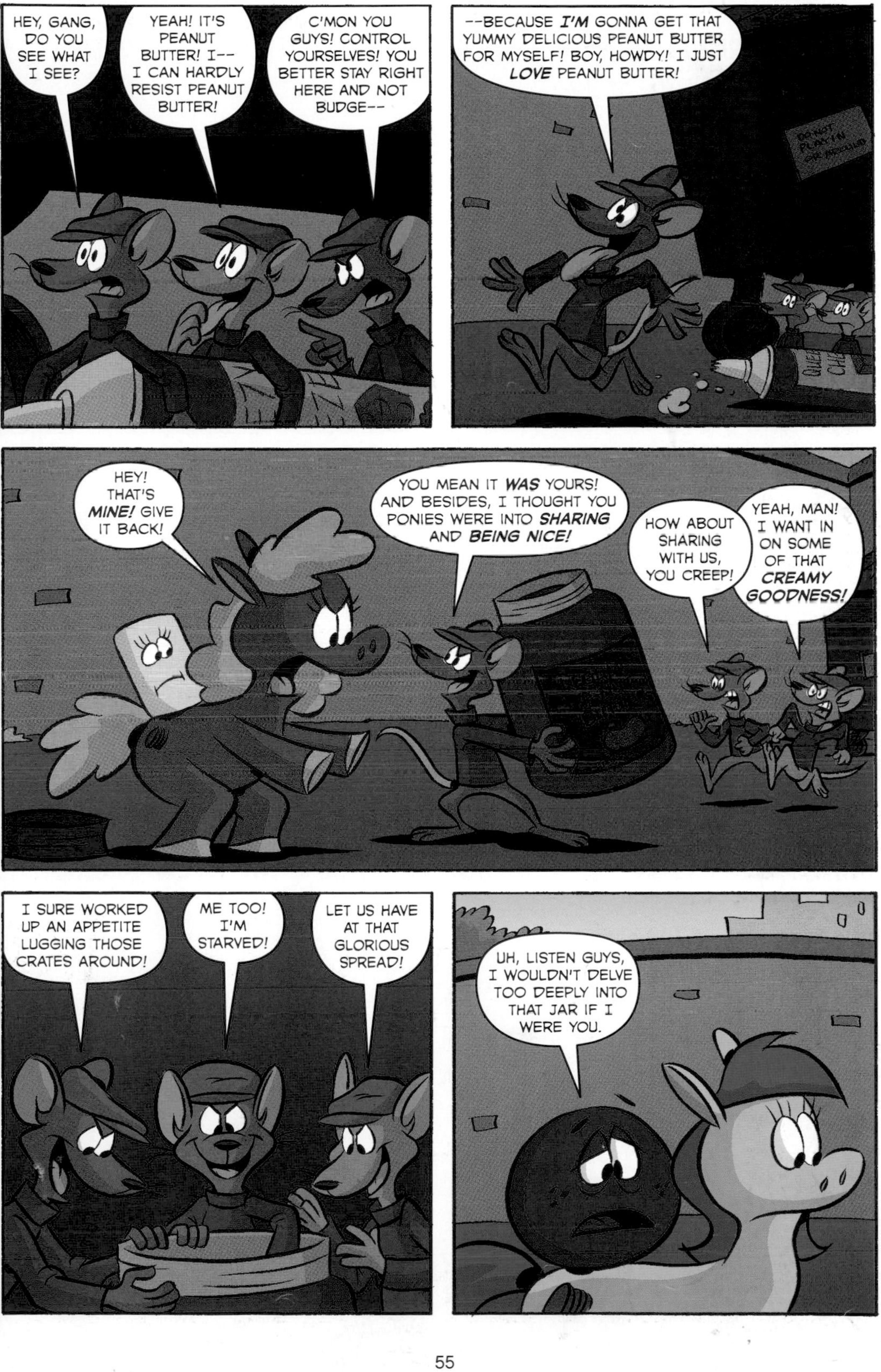
HEY, GANG, DO YOU SEE WHAT I SEE?
YEAH! IT'S PEANUT BUTTER! I-- I CAN HARDLY RESIST PEANUT BUTTER!
C'MON YOU GUYS! CONTROL YOURSELVES! YOU BETTER STAY RIGHT HERE AND NOT BUDGE--
--BECAUSE **I'M** GONNA GET THAT YUMMY DELICIOUS PEANUT BUTTER FOR MYSELF! BOY, HOWDY! I JUST **LOVE** PEANUT BUTTER!
HEY! THAT'S **MINE!** GIVE IT BACK!
YOU MEAN IT **WAS** YOURS! AND BESIDES, I THOUGHT YOU PONIES WERE INTO **SHARING** AND **BEING NICE!**
HOW ABOUT SHARING WITH US, YOU CREEP!
YEAH, MAN! I WANT IN ON SOME OF THAT **CREAMY GOODNESS!**
I SURE WORKED UP AN APPETITE LUGGING THOSE CRATES AROUND!
ME TOO! I'M STARVED!
LET US HAVE AT THAT GLORIOUS SPREAD!
UH, LISTEN GUYS, I WOULDN'T DELVE TOO DEEPLY INTO THAT JAR IF I WERE YOU.

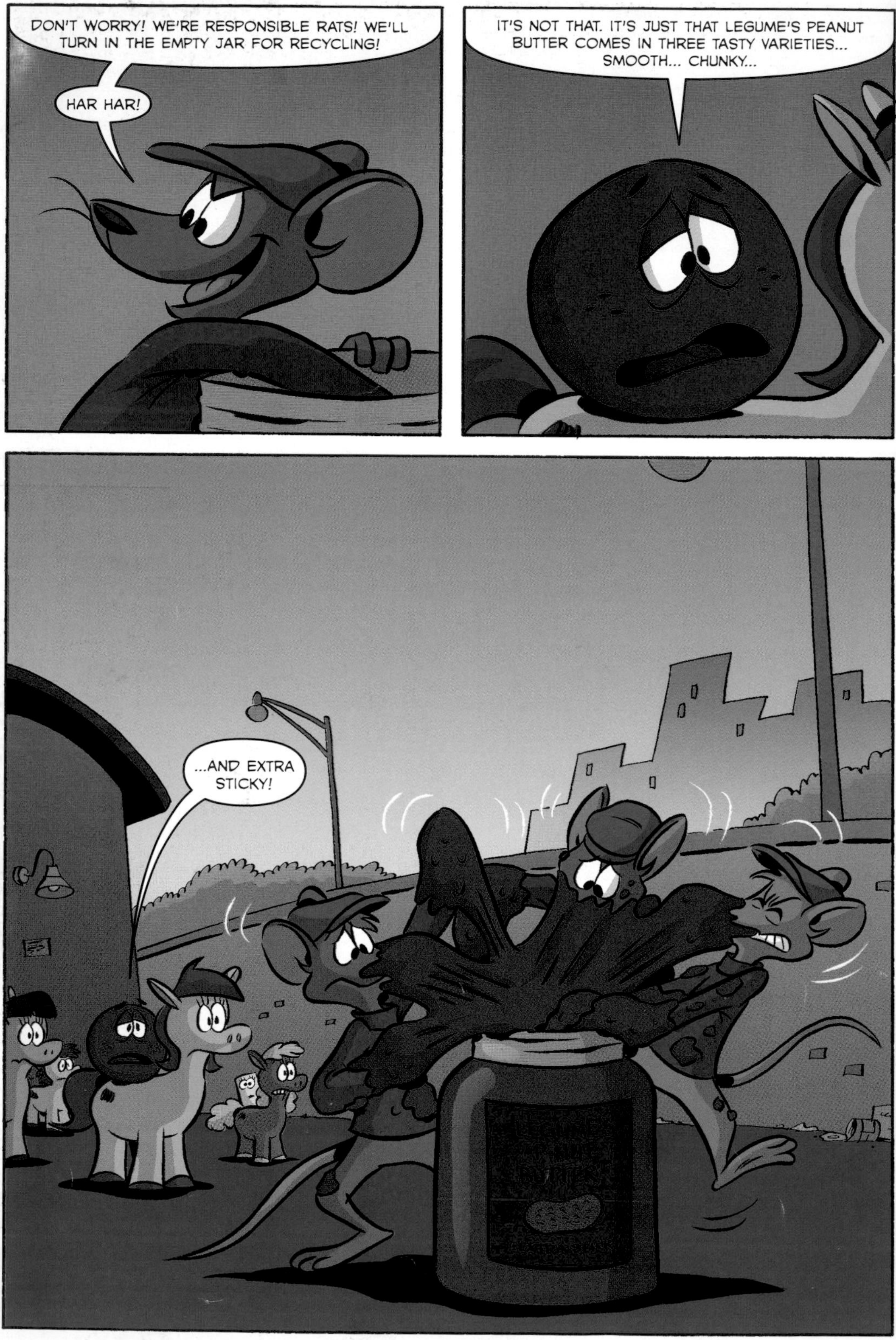
DON'T WORRY! WE'RE RESPONSIBLE RATS! WE'LL TURN IN THE EMPTY JAR FOR RECYCLING!
HAR HAR!
IT'S NOT THAT. IT'S JUST THAT LEGUME'S PEANUT BUTTER COMES IN THREE TASTY VARIETIES... SMOOTH... CHUNKY...
...AND EXTRA STICKY!

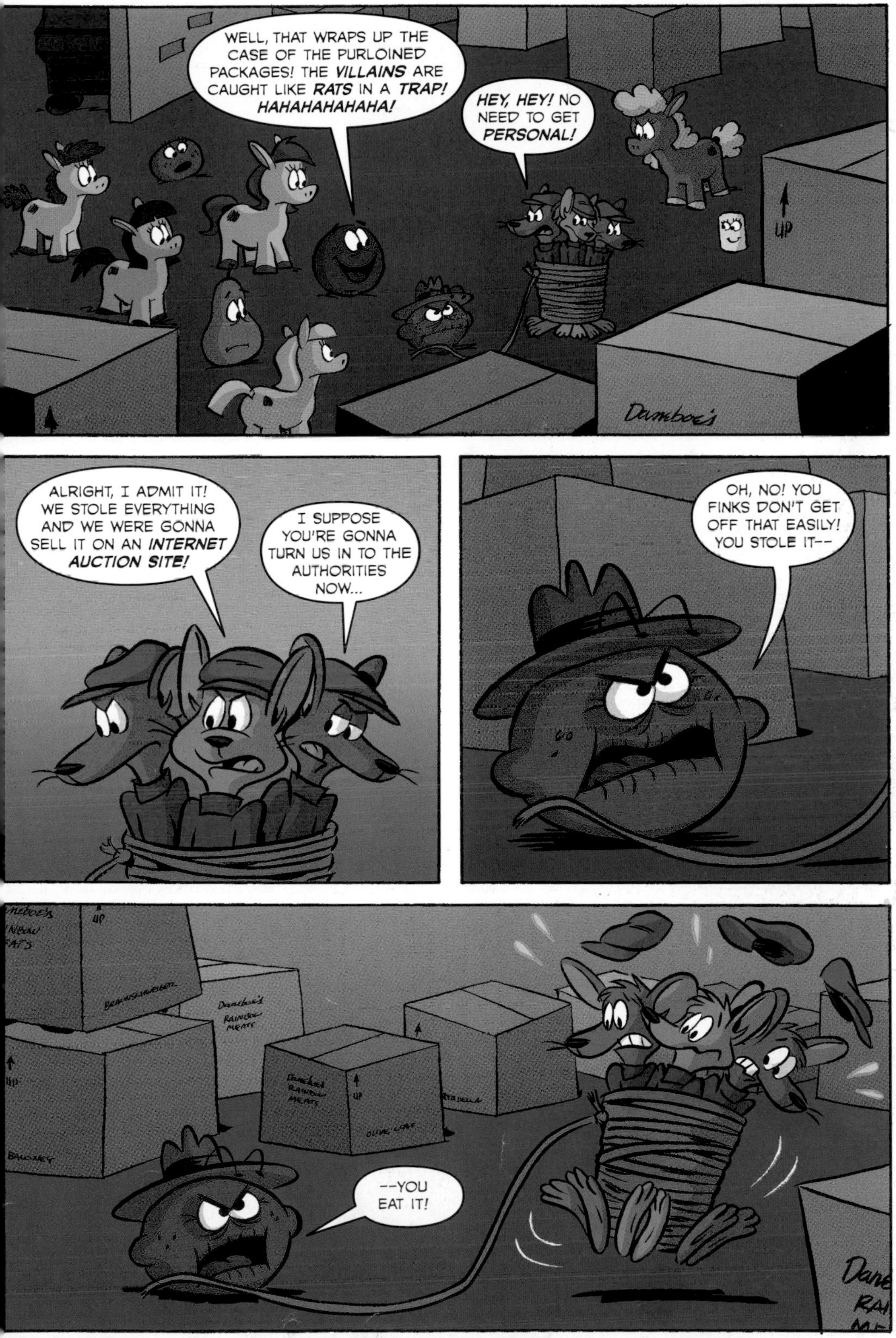
WELL, THAT WRAPS UP THE CASE OF THE PURLOINED PACKAGES! THE *VILLAINS* ARE CAUGHT LIKE *RATS* IN A *TRAP!* *HAHAHAHAHAHA!*
HEY, HEY! NO NEED TO GET *PERSONAL!*
ALRIGHT, I ADMIT IT! WE STOLE EVERYTHING AND WE WERE GONNA SELL IT ON AN *INTERNET AUCTION SITE!*
I SUPPOSE YOU'RE GONNA TURN US IN TO THE AUTHORITIES NOW...
OH, NO! YOU FINKS DON'T GET OFF THAT EASILY! YOU STOLE IT--
--YOU EAT IT!

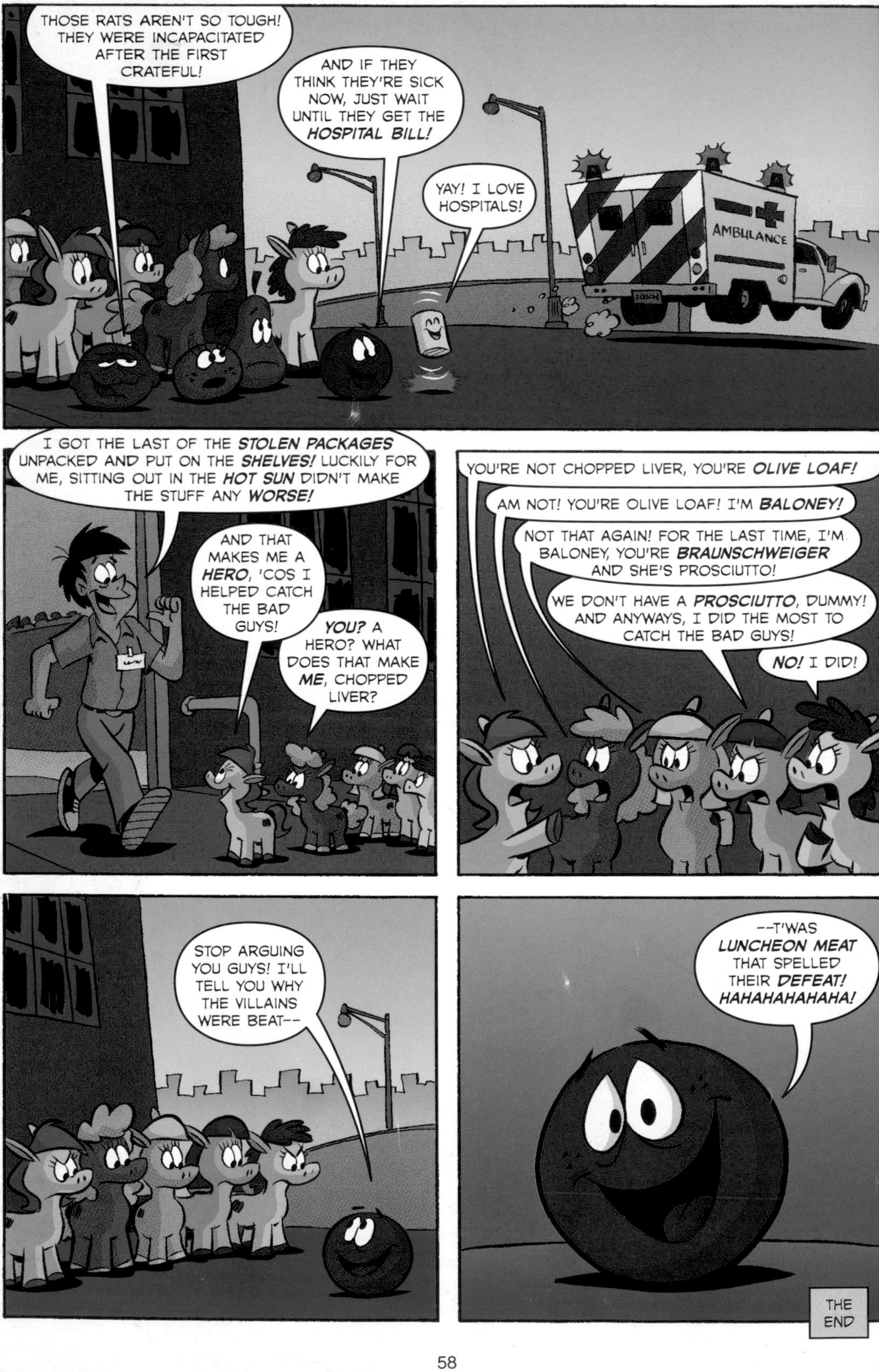
THOSE RATS AREN'T SO TOUGH! THEY WERE INCAPACITATED AFTER THE FIRST CRATEFUL!
AND IF THEY THINK THEY'RE SICK NOW, JUST WAIT UNTIL THEY GET THE *HOSPITAL BILL!*
YAY! I LOVE HOSPITALS!
AMBULANCE
I GOT THE LAST OF THE *STOLEN PACKAGES* UNPACKED AND PUT ON THE *SHELVES!* LUCKILY FOR ME, SITTING OUT IN THE *HOT SUN* DIDN'T MAKE THE STUFF ANY *WORSE!*
AND THAT MAKES ME A *HERO*, 'COS I HELPED CATCH THE BAD GUYS!
YOU? A HERO? WHAT DOES THAT MAKE *ME*, CHOPPED LIVER?
YOU'RE NOT CHOPPED LIVER, YOU'RE *OLIVE LOAF!*
AM NOT! YOU'RE OLIVE LOAF! I'M *BALONEY!*
NOT THAT AGAIN! FOR THE LAST TIME, I'M BALONEY, YOU'RE *BRAUNSCHWEIGER* AND SHE'S PROSCIUTTO!
WE DON'T HAVE A *PROSCIUTTO*, DUMMY! AND ANYWAYS, I DID THE MOST TO CATCH THE BAD GUYS!
NO! I DID!
STOP ARGUING YOU GUYS! I'LL TELL YOU WHY THE VILLAINS WERE BEAT--
--T'WAS *LUNCHEON MEAT* THAT SPELLED THEIR *DEFEAT! HAHAHAHAHAHA!*
THE END

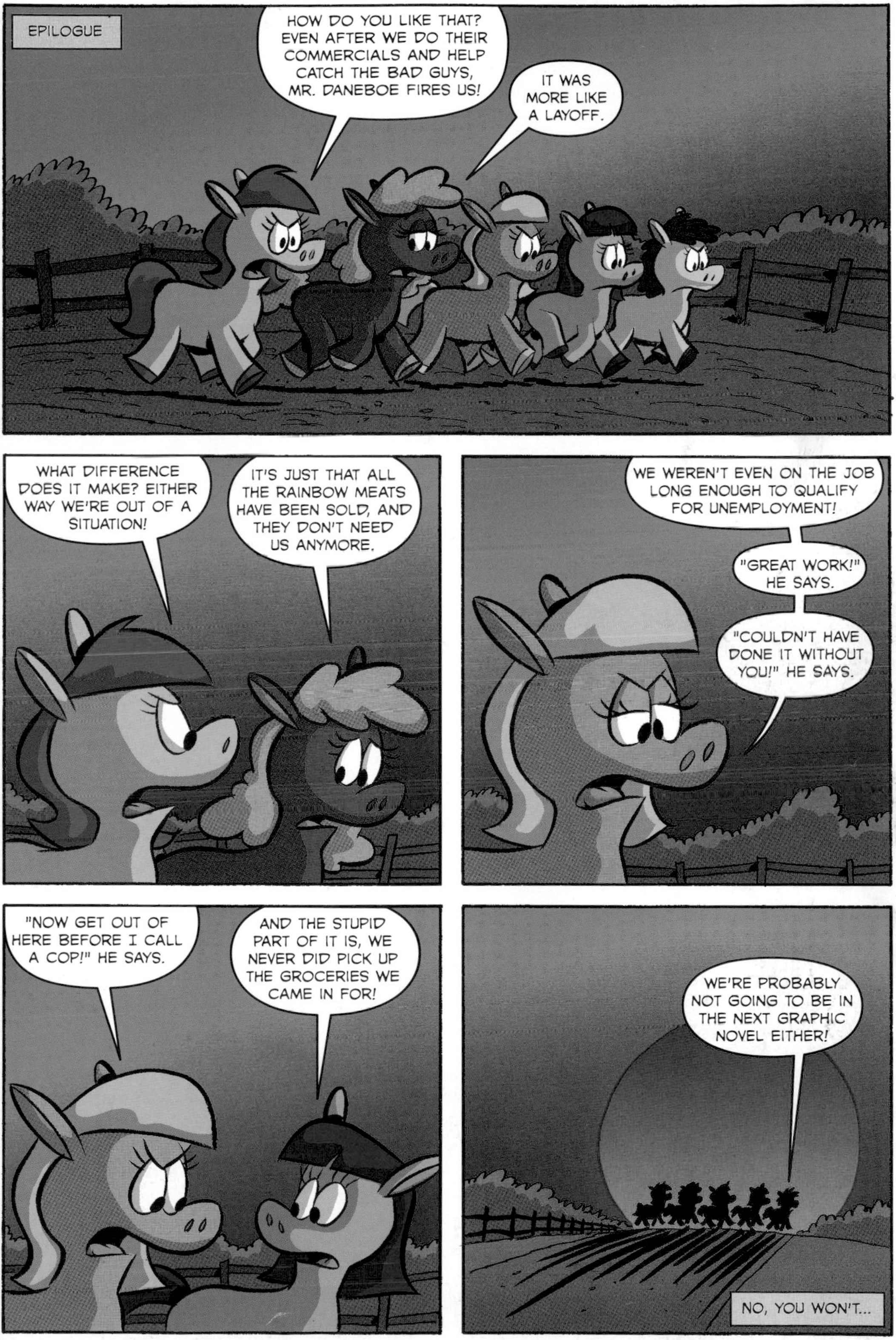
EPILOGUE
HOW DO YOU LIKE THAT? EVEN AFTER WE DO THEIR COMMERCIALS AND HELP CATCH THE BAD GUYS, MR. DANEBOE FIRES US!
IT WAS MORE LIKE A LAYOFF.
WHAT DIFFERENCE DOES IT MAKE? EITHER WAY WE'RE OUT OF A SITUATION!
IT'S JUST THAT ALL THE RAINBOW MEATS HAVE BEEN SOLD, AND THEY DON'T NEED US ANYMORE.
WE WEREN'T EVEN ON THE JOB LONG ENOUGH TO QUALIFY FOR UNEMPLOYMENT!
"GREAT WORK!" HE SAYS.
"COULDN'T HAVE DONE IT WITHOUT YOU!" HE SAYS.
"NOW GET OUT OF HERE BEFORE I CALL A COP!" HE SAYS.
AND THE STUPID PART OF IT IS, WE NEVER DID PICK UP THE GROCERIES WE CAME IN FOR!
WE'RE PROBABLY NOT GOING TO BE IN THE NEXT GRAPHIC NOVEL EITHER!
NO, YOU WON'T...

WATCH OUT FOR PAPERCUTZ™

Welcome to the somewhat-silly, yet strangely somber sixth and final ANNOYING ORANGE graphic novel from Papercutz, those nasty meat-eaters dedicated to publishing great graphic novels for all ages. I'm Jim Salicrup, the Editor-in-Chief here to confirm what has been kidded about here and there through-out this graphic novel-- this is indeed our final ANNOYING ORANGE graphic novel. As George Harrison sang, "All Things Must Pass," and this graphic novel series is no exception. But while the graphic novel series may be over, ANNOYING ORANGE lives on… right where he began on YouTube.com/realannoyingorange.

toto
1
TROUBLE
BACK TO CRASS
THIERRY COPPÉE
PAPERCUTZ

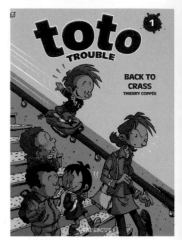

And Papercutz continues on as well! While LEGO® NINJAGO continues to top the New York Times Best-Selling Graphic Books list with every volume, we've also added some titles that we think ANNOYING ORANGE fans may appreciate as well! For general dumb humor and awful puns, may I direct your attention to TOTO TROUBLE by Thierry Coppée. Toto isn't the brightest kid around, but he can be a lot of fun, in his own way. Check out the preview pages starting on page 61. And if you enjoyed the "dinersaurs" in "Fruitstones, Meet the Fruitstones!" we suspect you may enjoy DINOSAURS #1 "In the Beginning" by Arnaud Plumeri and Bloz. In this graphic novel series, zany paleontologist (not to be confused with a Smurfologist) Indino Jones showcases all the latest and greatest facts about real-life dinosaurs! See the preview on page 63.

Plumeri & Bloz
Dinosaurs
IN THE BEGINNING...
PAPERCUTZ

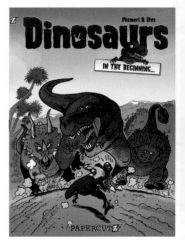

Before we conclude this graphic novel series, I wish to thank ANNOYING ORANGE creator Dane Boedigheimer for the opportunity to have fun creating comics based on his brainchild. Thanks, as always to Spencer Grove and Tom Sheppard. We'll all miss the *High Fructose Adventures of the Annoying Orange*. Also, I especially want to thank Mike Kazaleh and Scott Shaw! for somehow finding time to create the comics for this graphic novel series while they were also working away on the TV series. And while I wish both cartoonists all the best, I want Scott Shaw! to take extra-special care of himself! You wouldn't believe the health problems he's experienced recently—and we all want him to get as healthy as possible! Of course, I must also thank the ever-reliable and super-talented Laurie E. Smith! She's been coloring for Papercutz since there first was a Papercutz! Also thanks to letterers Chris Nelson, Janice Chiang, and even Tom Orzechowski! And finally, thanks to publisher Terry Nantier, Associate Editor Michael Petranek, and Production Coordinator Beth Scorzato—who all help make Papercutz a reality every day! And most of all—thanks to you! Without your support, we're nothing! It's greatly appreciated.

Thanks,

Jim

STAY IN TOUCH!

EMAIL:	salicrup@papercutz.com
WEB:	papercutz.com
TWITTER:	@papercutzgn
FACEBOOK:	PAPERCUTZGRAPHICNOVELS
REGULAR MAIL:	Papercutz, 160 Broadway, Suite 700, East Wing, New York, NY 10038

Special Preview of TOTO TROUBLE #1
"Back to Crass" by Thierry Coppée ...

"My Name is Toto"

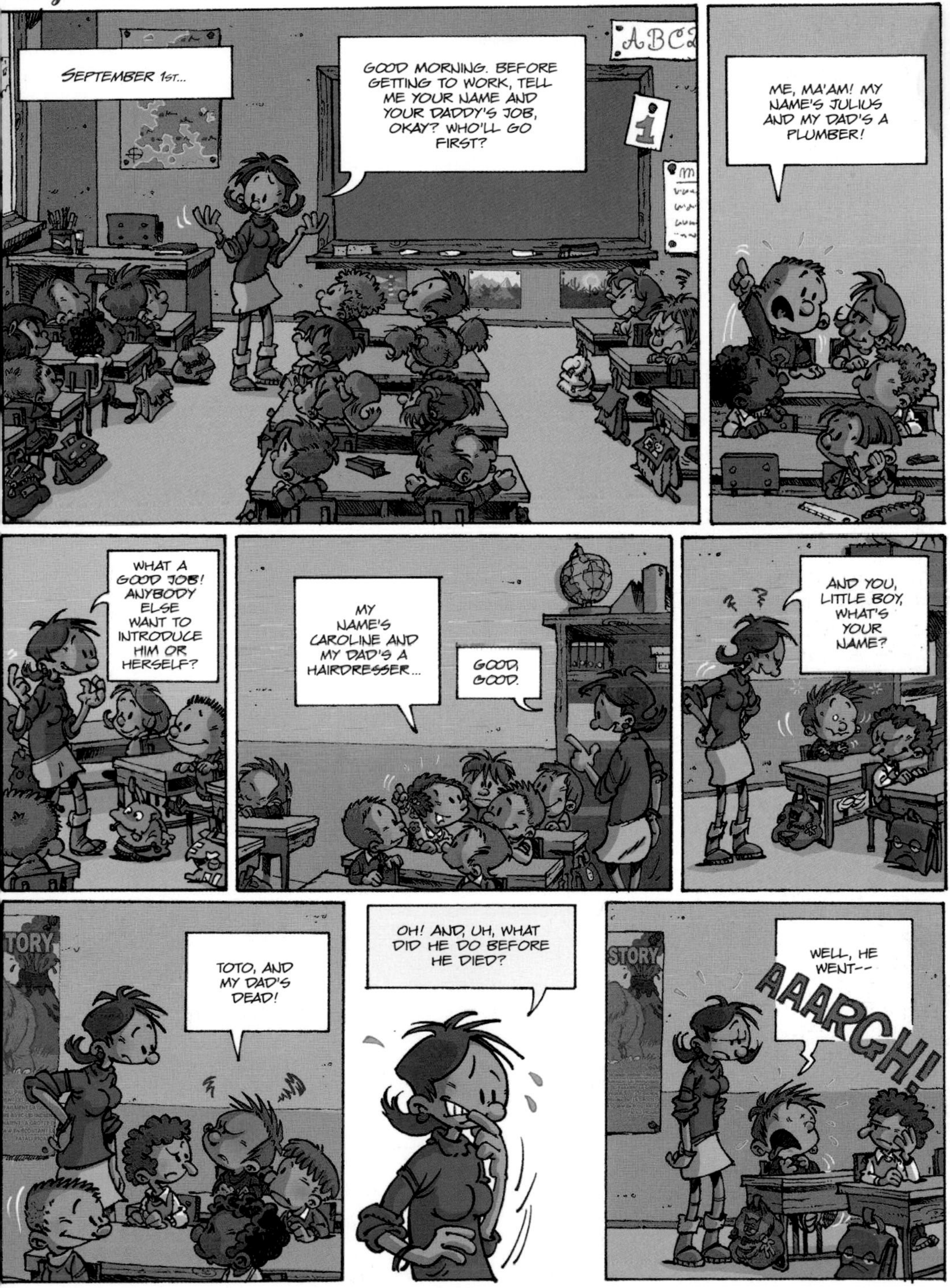
SEPTEMBER 1ST...
GOOD MORNING. BEFORE GETTING TO WORK, TELL ME YOUR NAME AND YOUR DADDY'S JOB, OKAY? WHO'LL GO FIRST?
ABC
ME, MA'AM! MY NAME'S JULIUS AND MY DAD'S A PLUMBER!
WHAT A GOOD JOB! ANYBODY ELSE WANT TO INTRODUCE HIM OR HERSELF?
MY NAME'S CAROLINE AND MY DAD'S A HAIRDRESSER...
GOOD, GOOD.
AND YOU, LITTLE BOY, WHAT'S YOUR NAME?
TOTO, AND MY DAD'S DEAD!
STORY
OH! AND, UH, WHAT DID HE DO BEFORE HE DIED?
WELL, HE WENT--
AAARGH!

"The Coffin"

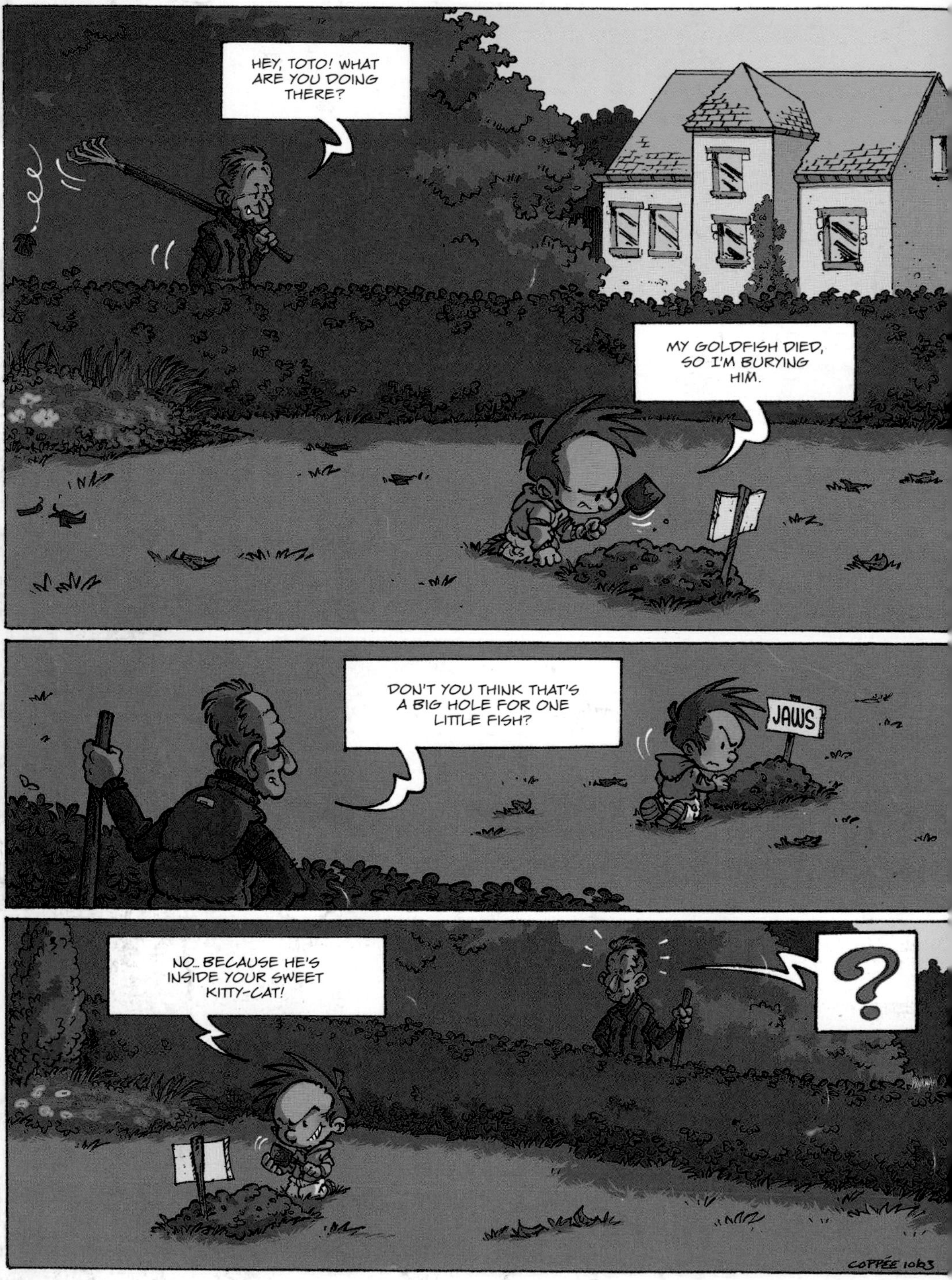
HEY, TOTO! WHAT ARE YOU DOING THERE?
MY GOLDFISH DIED, SO I'M BURYING HIM.
DON'T YOU THINK THAT'S A BIG HOLE FOR ONE LITTLE FISH?
JAWS
NO... BECAUSE HE'S INSIDE YOUR SWEET KITTY-CAT!
?
COPPÉE 10/03

Don't miss TOTO TROUBLE #1 "Back to Crass"!
Available now at booksellers everywhere!

Special preview of DINOSAURS #1
"In the Beginning" by Arnaud Plumeri and Bloz...

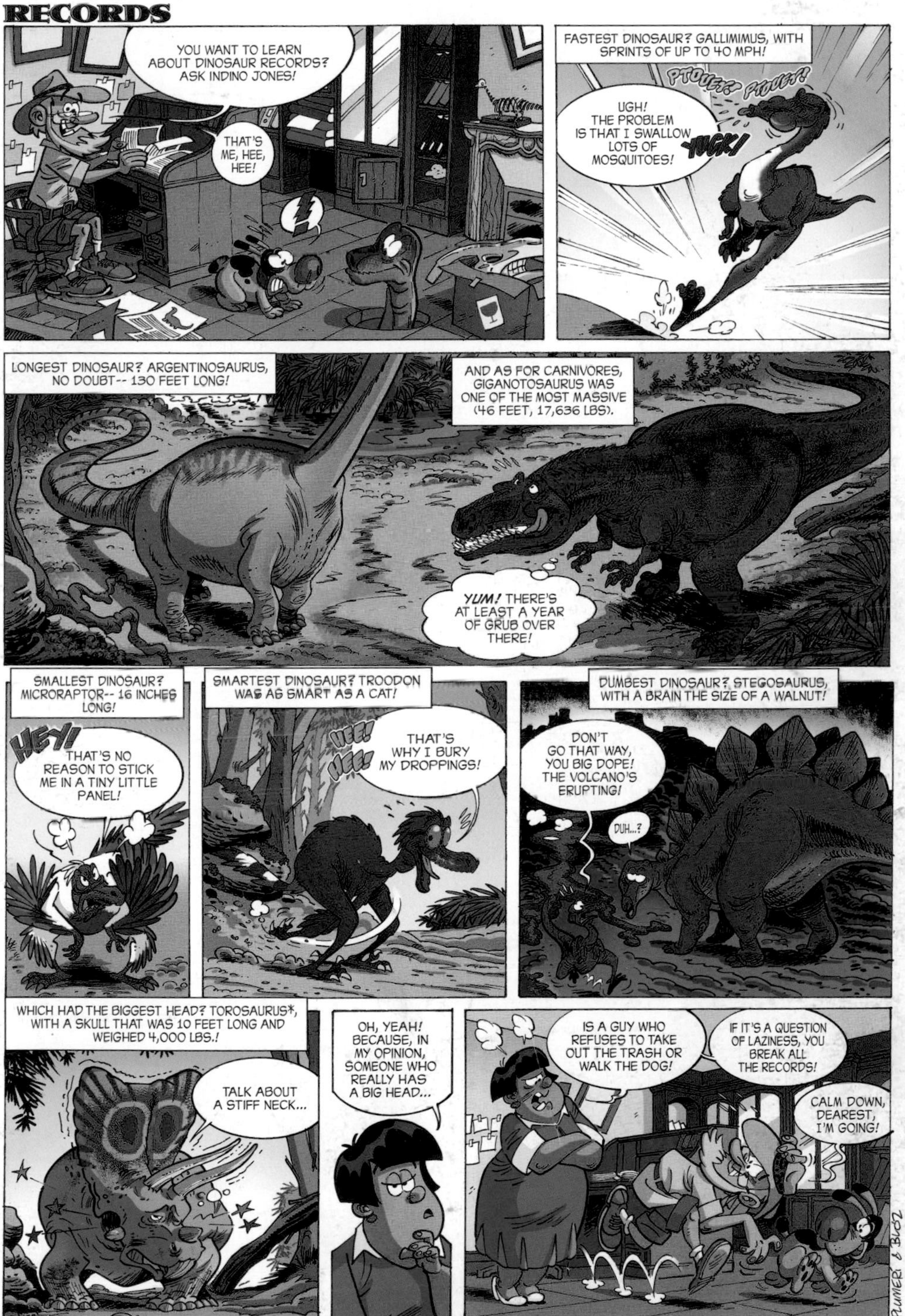
RECORDS
YOU WANT TO LEARN ABOUT DINOSAUR RECORDS? ASK INDINO JONES!
THAT'S ME, HEE, HEE!
FASTEST DINOSAUR? GALLIMIMUS, WITH SPRINTS OF UP TO 40 MPH!
UGH! THE PROBLEM IS THAT I SWALLOW LOTS OF MOSQUITOES!
YUCK!
LONGEST DINOSAUR? ARGENTINOSAURUS, NO DOUBT-- 130 FEET LONG!
AND AS FOR CARNIVORES, GIGANOTOSAURUS WAS ONE OF THE MOST MASSIVE (46 FEET, 17,636 LBS).
YUM! THERE'S AT LEAST A YEAR OF GRUB OVER THERE!
SMALLEST DINOSAUR? MICRORAPTOR-- 16 INCHES LONG!
HEY!
THAT'S NO REASON TO STICK ME IN A TINY LITTLE PANEL!
SMARTEST DINOSAUR? TROODON WAS AS SMART AS A CAT!
HEE! HEE!
THAT'S WHY I BURY MY DROPPINGS!
DUMBEST DINOSAUR? STEGOSAURUS, WITH A BRAIN THE SIZE OF A WALNUT!
DON'T GO THAT WAY, YOU BIG DOPE! THE VOLCANO'S ERUPTING!
DUH...?
WHICH HAD THE BIGGEST HEAD? TOROSAURUS*, WITH A SKULL THAT WAS 10 FEET LONG AND WEIGHED 4,000 LBS.!
TALK ABOUT A STIFF NECK...
OH, YEAH! BECAUSE, IN MY OPINION, SOMEONE WHO REALLY HAS A BIG HEAD...
IS A GUY WHO REFUSES TO TAKE OUT THE TRASH OR WALK THE DOG!
IF IT'S A QUESTION OF LAZINESS, YOU BREAK ALL THE RECORDS!
CALM DOWN, DEAREST, I'M GOING!
PLUMERI & BLOZ

*EXPERTS HAVE FOUND THAT TOROSAURUS MIGHT HAVE ACTUALLY BEEN AN ADULT TRICERATOPS.

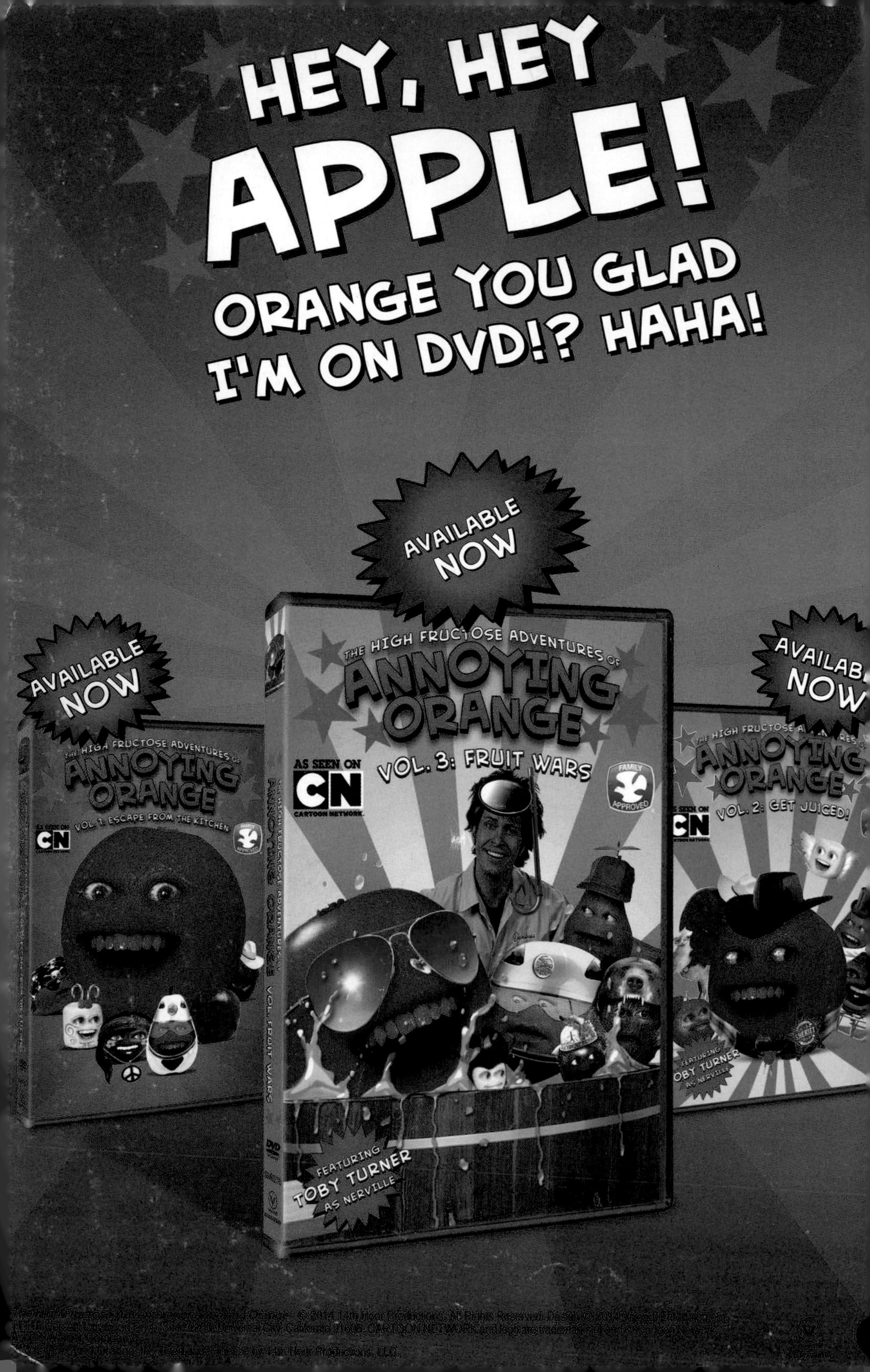
HEY, HEY
APPLE!
ORANGE YOU GLAD
I'M ON DVD!? HAHA!
AVAILABLE NOW
THE HIGH FRUCTOSE ADVENTURES OF
ANNOYING ORANGE
AS SEEN ON
CN
CARTOON NETWORK
VOL. 3: FRUIT WARS
FAMILY APPROVED
FEATURING
TOBY TURNER
AS NERVILLE
AVAILABLE NOW
THE HIGH FRUCTOSE ADVENTURES OF
ANNOYING ORANGE
VOL. 1: ESCAPE FROM THE KITCHEN
AVAILABLE NOW
ANNOYING ORANGE
VOL. 2: GET JUICED!